A MARRIAGE
WORTH SAVING

BY

THERESE BEHARRIE

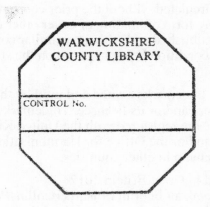

MILLS &
BOON

First published in Great Britain 2017
By Mills & Boon, an imprint of HarperCollins*Publishers*
1 London Bridge Street, London, SE1 9GF

Large Print edition 2017

© 2017 Therese Beharrie

ISBN: 978-0-263-07152-8

Printed and bound in Great Britain
by CPI Antony Rowe, Chippenham, Wiltshire

To my husband, Grant. Thank you for showing me what a strong relationship is. It's knowing that we can face whatever comes our way that has helped me to write about a relationship that survives after the unthinkable. You are my inspiration.
I love you.

And for the incredibly strong women in my family.

Your courage in facing the most heartbreaking of losses inspired this story. Your determination in facing the future inspired these characters.
I hope it brings you a measure of comfort.

PROLOGUE

JORDAN THOMAS COULDN'T take his eyes off his event planner.

Well, he supposed he couldn't exactly call her 'his' when his father had been the one to hire her. But since he had inherited his mother's half of the vineyard—which he would have gladly traded to have her back—he figured his father's decision went for the both of them.

'Are you going to keep staring at her, or are you going to introduce yourself?'

His father, Gregory, barely glanced at him as he said the words. The serious tone Greg had used would have alarmed anyone who didn't know him—would have made him seem almost angry—but at twenty-seven years old Jordan knew the nuances of his father's voice. Greg was baiting him.

'I'm still thinking about it. I'm not sure I want

to bother her an hour before the event,' Jordan answered.

When his father didn't reply, he sighed.

'Maybe you should call her over so that I can introduce myself, Dad.'

His father nodded his approval. 'Mila! Would you come over here for a second?'

The minute she started walking towards them, Jordan's heart raced. She was absolutely beautiful, he thought as he took in the perfectly designed features of her face. A small nose led to luscious lips, pink as a cherry blossom and which curved into a smile when she saw his father. The smile kicked his heart up another notch even though her brown eyes watched him carefully, surrounded by the fullest, darkest eyelashes he had ever seen.

He wondered idly if they were like that with help from cosmetic enhancements, but something told him that everything about her was natural. She made him think of the fields where his grapes grew in the vineyard—of the vibrancy of their colours and the feeling of home he always felt looking at it.

He didn't have time to ponder the unsettling thought when she stopped in front of them.

'Mila, you haven't had the chance to meet my son yet.' Greg nudged Jordan, and if Jordan hadn't been so mesmerised by the woman in front of him, he might have wondered at his father pushing him towards her.

But all thoughts flew out of his head the minute he introduced himself and she said, 'Mila Dennis,' and took his outstretched hand.

He'd thought there would be heat—a natural reaction to touching someone he found attractive. But he hadn't expected the heat to burn through his entire body. He hadn't expected the longing that curled in his stomach, the desire to make her his. But most of all he hadn't expected the pull that he felt towards her—a connection that went beyond the physical.

She pulled her hand away quickly, tucking a non-existent piece of hair behind her ear, and he knew she had felt it, too.

'It's lovely to meet you, Mr Thomas.'

Her voice sounded like music to him and he frowned, wondering at his reaction to a woman he hadn't even known for five minutes.

'Jordan, please. Mr Thomas is my father.' He shoved his hands into his pockets and watched as a smile spread across Greg's face. Jordan felt his eyebrows raise.

'Actually, Mila doesn't call me that,' Greg said, and Jordan realised Greg's smile was aimed at Mila. It was a sign of affection that made their relationship seem more than that of employer/ employee. It was almost...*familial*. Almost, because Greg didn't even share his smiles—a rare commodity—with his family. With his son.

He would have to ask his father about it, Jordan thought when Mila's lips curved in response. But then she looked at Jordan and the smile faltered.

'Well, I think it's best that I get back. We have hundreds of people coming today. It was a great idea to host a Valentine's Day Under the Stars event.'

'It was mine.' Jordan wasn't sure why he said it, but he wanted her to know that *he* was responsible for the idea that had brought the two of them together.

He had a feeling it would be significant.

'Well, it was a great one.' She frowned, as though she wasn't sure how to respond to him.

'I'll see you both a little later then. Greg...' She smiled at Jordan's father, but again it faltered when she turned her attention to him. 'Jordan...'

She said his name carefully, as though it was a minefield she was navigating through. He watched her, saw the flash of awareness and then denial in her eyes, and something settled inside him.

'What was *that*?'

His father had waited for Mila to leave before asking, and Jordan turned to him, noting the carefully blank expression on Greg's face.

'I think I've just met the woman I'm going to spend the rest of my life with.'

Greg's eyebrows rose so high they disappeared under the hair that had fallen over his forehead. And then came another nod of approval.

'I *knew* you were a smart boy,' he said, and a warm feeling spread through Jordan's heart at what he knew was high praise coming from his father.

Meeting Jordan Thomas had unsettled Mila so much that she'd almost lost her headline act.

When she heard the commotion in the tent

they'd set up behind the amphitheatre stage—
and saw the sympathetic look Lulu, her assistant and long-time friend, shot her on her way
towards the sound—Mila knew she was about
to walk into a drama.

'Why would you do this to me on Valentine's
Day?' Karen, the pretty singer that the whole of
South Africa had been raving about since she'd
won the biggest singing competition in the coun-
try, was wailing. 'You couldn't wait *one day* before breaking up with me? And right before a
performance, too!'

Wails turned into heart-wrenching sobs—the
kind that could only come from a teenage girl
losing her first love—and Mila felt the telltale
tickling of the start of a headache. She took in
the chagrined look on Karen's guitarist's face and
realised he was responsible for the tears.

She sighed, and then strode to the little crowd
where the scene was unfolding.

'What's going on?'

'Kevin broke up with me!' Karen said through
her sobs, and Mila wondered why she had decided that hiring a fresh young girl to perform at
one of the biggest events she had ever planned—

for one of the most prominent clients she had ever worked for—had seemed like a good idea.

And then she remembered the voice in the online videos she'd watched of Karen, and the number of views all those videos had got, and she sighed again.

'On *Valentine's Day*, Kevin?' Mila asked, instead of voicing the 'What were you thinking?' that sat on the tip of her tongue. Best not to rock the boat any further, she thought. Kevin, who looked to be only a couple of years older than the girl whose heart he had broken, shifted uncomfortably on his feet.

'Well, ma'am, there was this—'

He cut himself off when Mila held up her hand, affronted that he was calling her 'ma'am' even though she was only a few years older than him. Four, max. She'd also realised that whatever Kevin had been about to say would have caused Karen even more distress.

'Okay, everyone, the show is over. Can we all get back to what we need to be doing? Our guests are starting to arrive,' Mila called out and then waited until everyone had scattered, eyeing those who lingered so that they eventually left, too.

When she was alone with Karen, she turned and took the girl's hand. 'Have you ever been broken up with before, Karen?'

Red curls bounced as Karen shook her head, and Mila suddenly felt all the sympathy in the world for her.

'It sucks. It really does. Your heart feels like it's been ripped into two and your stomach is in twists. It doesn't matter when it happens—that feeling is always the same. Stays there, too, if you let it.'

Mila thought about when she had been Karen's age—of how moving from foster home to foster home had meant that she'd never had someone to tell her this the first time a boy had broken *her* heart—and said what she'd wished she'd known then.

'But, you know, the older you get, the more you realise that the less it meant, the less it will hurt. And, since Kevin over there seems like a bit of a jerk, I'm thinking you'll be over this in a week…maybe two.'

'Really?' The hope in Karen's eyes made Mila smile.

'I'm pretty sure. And, you know, the best re-

venge is to prove to him that it didn't really matter that much after all.'

'But how…? Oh, if I perform with him, he'll
think that I've got over it. Maybe he'll even want
me back!'

She said the words with such enthusiasm that
Mila resisted rolling her eyes. 'Sure… Why not?'

She watched Karen run to the bathroom to
freshen up, feeling both relieved that Karen was
going to perform and annoyed that she didn't
seem to have heard a word Mila had told her.

'That was pretty impressive.'

The deep, intensely male voice sent shivers
up Mila's spine, and she turned slowly to face
its owner. Jordan Thomas's eyes were the most
captivating she had ever seen—a combination
of gold and brown that made her think of the
first signs of autumn. They made the masculine
features of his face seem ordinary though she
knew that, based on the way he made her feel
distinctly female, he was anything *but* ordinary.
Light brown hair lay shaggy over his forehead, as
though he had forgotten to comb it, but it added
a charm to his face that might have been otherwise lost under the pure maleness of him.

She took a moment to compose herself, and then she smiled at him.

Because she was a professional and he was a client.

And because she needed to prove that the effect he'd had on her when they'd first met had been a fluke.

'Thanks. All a part of the job.'

'Consoling teenage girls is a part of your job?'

The smile came more naturally now. 'When the teenage girl is the headline act at my event, yes.'

He shoved his hands into his pockets and the action drew her attention to the muscles under the black T-shirt he wore. Heaven help her, but she actually thought about running her hands over them before she could stop herself.

'It looks great.'

She blinked, and then realised that he was talking about the event. She nodded, and then peeked out of the tent to where people were beginning to fill the seats of the amphitheatre.

'It's come along nicely.' She noted that the wine stalls were already busy, and she could smell the waft of food from the food vendors.

'You should pat yourself on the back. It *was* your idea after all.'

She glanced back at him, saw the slow, sexy smile spread on his face, and thought that she needed to get away from him as she had almost fanned herself.

'It may have been my idea to host the event here at the vineyard, but I could never have arranged a concert *and* a movie screening in one night.'

'It pulls in fans for the concert and romantics for the movie,' she said, as she had to Greg Thomas so many times before. 'Who can resist either of those events—or any event, really—under the stars, with delicious Thomas Vineyard wines on tap, on the most romantic day of the year?'

His eyes sparkled, as though her words had given him some kind of idea, and then he smiled at her. A full smile that was more impactful than a thousand of his slow, sexy ones.

'I need to check everything one more time. If you'll excuse me?'

Jordan nodded, and then said, 'I'll find you later.'

She frowned as she walked away, wondering what on earth he'd meant by that.

When the movie was about ten minutes in, she found out.

He had come to her and claimed that there was a problem with the wine delivery for those who had pre-ordered boxes to take home with them. Like a fool she had followed him, her mind racing to a million different ways of solving the problem. Only when he led her through a gate past the Thomas house did it occur to her that there might not be an emergency.

'What is this?' she asked quietly, even though they were far enough away from the guests that no one would hear her.

'It's a picnic. Under the stars.'

A part of her melted at that—the pure romance of it made her feel as giddy as a girl on her first date. But it didn't change the way her heart raced in panic as she took in the scene in front of her.

A blanket was spread out overlooking the vineyard, and in the moonlight she could see the shadow of the mountains. For a brief moment she wondered what it would look like during the day, with its colours and its magnitude and the welcoming silence.

She shook her head and looked at what was spread on the blanket. A bottle of wine—she couldn't read the label, though she thought she saw the Thomas Vineyard crest—cooled in an ice bucket with two glasses next to it. A variety of the foods that she hadn't had time to taste accompanied the wine.

Although she really didn't want to, she found herself softening even more, her heart racing now for completely different reasons than a man expressing interest in her.

'Are you going to stay or run?'

She looked up at him, and though his words sounded playful, his expression told her otherwise.

'Are those my only two options?'

'I could offer you another.'

She saw the change in his eyes and her body heated.

'What would you do if I ran?' she asked, hoping to distract him.

'I'd run with you.'

She resisted the urge to smile at his charm,

and wondered why someone like Jordan Thomas would be interested in her? First, she was his employee. And second, she didn't have much to offer him. What could a woman with no family and no foundation offer a man like Jordan Thomas of the Thomas Vineyard?

Still, she found herself saying, 'Pour me a glass of wine, Jordan.'

He handed her a glass with a smile that had her shaking her head.

'You don't agree with my methods?'

'You mean lying to get me to share a drink with you?'

'Yes.' He grinned. 'But you can't tell me this isn't a welcome change to having to run around all day?'

'No, I can't.' She sighed, and took a sip from her wine. 'Drinking wine after a long day with a handsome man should be the only way to unwind.'

She didn't realise what she'd said until she saw him smiling at her, and then she blushed furiously.

Where had that come from?

'I didn't mean—'

'To tell me I'm handsome?'

She set her wine down. 'Yes. It's been a long day.'

'So I could ask you anything now and you would answer it?'

'Maybe,' she said softly, caught by the expression in his eyes.

And then she wondered who this person who was flirting with this gorgeous man was. Because surely it couldn't be tame, safe Mila. How often had she heard those comments from boys she had dated? From her foster siblings, who'd had no interest in hanging out with a girl who couldn't bring herself to try drugs or go out drinking every night, no matter how desperately she'd wanted to be liked?

She closed her eyes at the pain, and picked up her wine glass again. It must have been the stress of the event that had her thinking about a past she'd thought she'd left behind.

But before she could drink her wine, Jordan took the glass out of her hand and she froze.

'Do you have a boyfriend?' he asked her, and she realised he was a lot closer than he'd been a few moments ago. Her throat dried at the woodsy smell that filled her senses, and suddenly she wished she hadn't flirted with him.

'No,' she answered quickly, her breathing becoming more heavy than she thought could be healthy.

'Good. That makes this much easier.'

'What are you talking about?' She couldn't take her eyes off him, and knew she should be worried that the realisation only caused the slightest bit of alarm in her.

'Us.' He pulled the clip out of her hair so that it fell to her shoulders. 'I'm glad you won't have to break another man's heart so that we can be together.'

'That's presumptuous of you,' she replied, though for the life of her, she couldn't think of one reason why that was a problem. Even when he had her speaking her mind without the filter she usually employed with every word.

He didn't respond immediately, and she wondered if she'd said something wrong.

And then her heart stopped completely when his hand stilled on her neck and he said, 'It should be. Everything inside me is saying that feeling this way about someone without even knowing them is crazy. And yet I can't help myself.'

His hand moved to her face, and she thought that even if the sky fell down on them she wouldn't be able to look away from him.

'So tell me whether I'm being presumptuous when I say I know you feel it, too?'

She couldn't speak because the pieces that had been floating around in her head since they'd met—and the feelings that had become unsettled the moment he'd introduced himself—told her there was truth to his words.

'You did all of this to…to see if I felt the same way?'

'No.' He smiled, and tucked a piece of hair behind her ear. 'I did this to make you realise that you *did*.'

'Jordan, I—'

His lips were suddenly on hers, and she felt herself melt, felt her resistance—her denial— fade away. Because as his mouth moved against hers, her heart was telling her that it wanted to be with him. She ignored the way her mind told her she was being ridiculous, and instead ran her hands over the muscles she had admired earlier.

With one arm he moved everything that was on the blanket away and she found herself on her back, with Jordan's body half over hers. But she pulled away, her chest heaving as though she'd run a marathon.

'This is crazy,' she said shakily, but didn't move any further.

'Yes, it is,' he replied, his eyes filled with a mixture of desire and tenderness.

She raised a hand to his face, pushing his hair back and settling it on his cheek. He turned his head and kissed her hand. And in that moment, under the stars that sparkled brightly on Valentine's Day, she realised that she might have just fallen in love with a man she had only known for a few hours.

Even as her mind called her foolish she was pulling his lips back down to hers.

CHAPTER ONE

Two years later

JORDAN STOOD OUTSIDE his childhood home and grief—and guilt—crashed through him.

The house was like many he had seen in the Stellenbosch wine lands—large and white, with a black roof and shutters. Except he had grown up in this house. He'd played on the patio that stretched out in front of the house, with its stone pillars that had vines crawling up them. He and his father had spent Sunday evenings watching the sun set—usually in silence—on the rocking chairs that stood next to the large wooden door.

He turned his back on the house and the memories, and looked out to the gravel road that led to the rest of the vineyard.

Trees reached out to one another over the road, the colour of their leaves fading from the bright green of summer to the warm hues of autumn.

From where he stood he could see the chapel where he'd married Mila just three months after they'd met.

He shook his head. He wouldn't think about that now.

Instead he looked under the potted plants that lined the pathway to the front door for the key he knew his father had kept there. When he found it he began to walk to his father's house—except that wasn't true any more. He clenched his jaw at the reminder of the new ownership of the house—the house he had grown up in—and the reason he was back, and turned the key in the lock.

He heard it first—the crackling sound of fire blazing—and he set his bags down and hurried to the living room where he was sure he would find the house burning. And slowed when he realised that the fire was safely in the fireplace.

He turned his head to the couch in front of the fire, and his heart stopped when he saw his ex-wife sitting in front of it.

'What are *you* doing here?' he demanded before he could think, the shock of seeing her here, in his childhood home, forcing him to speak before he could think it through.

She jumped when she heard him, and shame poured through him as the glass of wine in her hand dropped to the ground and the colour seeped from her face.

'Jordan... What...? I...'

In another world, at another time, he might have found her stammering amusing. Now, though, he clamped down the emotions that filled him and asked again, 'What are you doing here, Mila?'

Her fingers curled at her sides—the only indication that she was fighting to gain her composure. He waited, giving her time to do so, perhaps to make up for startling her earlier.

'What are *you* doing here?' she asked him instead, crossing her arms and briefly drawing his attention to her chest. He shook his head and remembered how long it had taken him to realise that she took that stance whenever she felt threatened.

'You want to know why *I'm* here? In *my* father's home?'

'It's not your father's home any more, Jordan.'

His heart thudded. 'Is that why you're here? Because you'll own part of this house soon?'

She winced, and it made him think that maybe he wasn't the only one unhappy with his father's will.

'No, of course not. But I do live here.'

'What?'

The little colour she had left in her face faded, but her eyes never left his. If he hadn't been so shocked he might have been impressed at her guts. But his mind was still very much focused on her revelation.

'I live here,' she repeated. The shakiness in her voice wasn't completely gone, but the silken tone of it came through stronger. The tone that sounded like music when she laughed. That had once caressed his skin when she said, 'I love you.' The tone that had said 'I do!' two years ago as though nothing could touch them or their love.

How little they had known then...

He pushed the memories away.

'I heard that. I want to know why,' he said through clenched teeth, his temper precariously close to snapping.

'Because your father asked me to move in with him after...after everything that happened.'

The reminder of the past threatened to gut him, but he ignored it. 'So after we got divorced you thought it would be a good idea to move in with my father?'

'No, *he* did,' she said coldly, and again shame nudged him for reasons he didn't understand. 'He wanted—he *needed* someone around when you left.'

'And you agreed?'

'After his first heart attack, yes.'

Her words cut right through to his heart, and he asked the question despite the fact that everything inside him wanted to ignore it. 'His first? You mean his *only.*'

Something flashed through her eyes, and he wondered if it was sympathy. 'No, I mean his first. The one that killed him was his third.'

Jordan resisted the urge to close his eyes, to absorb the pain her words brought. He wondered how he had gone to his father's funeral, how he had spoken to the few friends Greg had had left, and was only hearing about this now.

But then, was it any wonder? a voice asked

him. His father had always kept his feelings to himself, not wanting to burden Jordan with them. An after-effect of *that* night, Jordan thought. But there was a part of him that wondered if Greg hadn't told him as punishment for Jordan leaving, even after his father had warned him that it would destroy his marriage—which it had. After Jordan had decided that limited contact with his father during the year he'd been gone—grief snapped at him when he thought that it had actually been the year before his father's death—was the only way he would be able to forget about what had happened...

'Why didn't you tell me?' he asked, determined not to get sucked in by his thoughts.

'He didn't want you to know.'

It was like a punch to the gut—and it told him that his father wanting to punish him might not have been such a farfetched conclusion.

'He told you that, or *you* decided it?'

Mila's face was clear, but when she spoke her voice was ice. 'It was Greg's decision. Do you think your father's friends would have kept quiet about it for *me*?'

She waited for his answer, but it didn't come. He was too busy processing her words.

'He didn't want you to come home until *you'd* decided to.'

'You should have called me,' he said, his voice low, dangerous.

'If you hadn't been so determined to put as much distance between us as possible—if you hadn't let it cloud your judgement—you would have *known* that you should have come home even though I didn't call you.'

Her voice was a mirror of his own thoughts, and if her words hadn't pierced his heart Jordan might have taken a moment to enjoy—perhaps a better word was *admire*—this new edge to Mila. But he was too distracted by the emotion that what she'd said had awoken in him.

Had his desire to escape the pain of his marriage blinded him to what he should have known? That he should have come home?

'So you're back because of the will?'

Her question drew him out of his thoughts—drew his attention to her. He took a moment before he answered her.

'Yes, that sped up my return to Cape Town. But I'm here for good.'

Jordan watched as her left hand groped behind her, and he moved when he realised she was looking for something to keep her standing. He caught her as she staggered back, his arm curved around her waist. His heartbeat was faster than it had been in a long time, and somewhere in the back of his mind he wondered if he'd really wanted to stop her from falling, or if he'd put himself in this awkward situation because...

He stopped thinking as he looked into those hauntingly beautiful eyes of hers that widened as they looked up at him. The love that had filled them a long time ago had been replaced by such a complexity of emotion that he could only see surprise there. And caution.

Her brown curls were tied back into a ponytail, making her delicate features seem sharper than they'd once been. But maybe that was because her face had lost its gentle rounding, he thought, and saw for the first time that she'd lost weight. Pressed against hers, his body acknowledged that her body felt different from what he remembered. The curves he'd enjoyed during their marriage were now more toned than before.

He wished he could say he didn't like it, but the way his body tightened told him that he would be lying if he did. The lips he had always been greedy for parted, and his eyes lowered. Electricity snapped between them as he thought about tasting her, about quenching the thirst that had burned inside him since they'd been apart...

They both pulled away at the same time, and again Jordan heard the smash of glass against the floor. Pieces of a wine bottle lay mingled with pieces of the glass Mila had dropped earlier, and Jordan belatedly realised that he'd knocked it over when he'd moved back.

'I'll get something for that,' she said, hurrying away before he could respond. But she didn't move fast enough for him to miss the flush on her face.

He stared at the mess on the floor—the mess they'd made within their first minutes of reuniting—and hoped it wasn't an omen for the rest of the time they'd spend together.

Mila grabbed the broom from the kitchen cupboard, and then stilled. She should take a moment to compose herself. Her hands were still shaking from the shock of seeing Jordan, and now her body was heated from their contact.

She hated that reminder of what he could do to her. Hated it even more that he could *still* do it to her, even after everything that had happened between them.

Why had he touched her anyway? She hadn't been going to fall—she was pretty sure about that. It had just been the prospect of him stay-ing—her stomach still churned at the thought—that had shaken her balance. And then, before she'd known it, she'd been in his arms, feeling comfort—and something else that she didn't care to admit—for the first time since the accident that had ruined their lives.

She took a deep breath and, when she was sure she was as prepared as she could be to face him again, she returned to the living room.

And felt her breath hitch again when she saw him standing there.

He was leaner now, though his body was still strong, with muscles clearly defined beneath his clothing. Perhaps there were more muscles now, whatever excess weight there had been once now firm. His hair was shorter, though it was still shaggy, falling lazily over his forehead as though begging to be pushed aside. And then there was his face...those beautiful planes drawn into the serious expression she was becoming accustomed to.

'We need to do something about the house,' he said when he saw her, and moved to take the cleaning items away from her.

But he stopped when he saw the expression in her eyes—the coldness she had become so used to aiming at him to protect herself from pain—and she bent to pick up the pieces of glass.

'I'll be leaving in the morning,' she said, grateful that he couldn't see her face as she tidied up.

The idea of going back to the house that reminded her of all that she'd had—and all that she'd lost—made her feel sick. But what choice did she have?

After Jordan had left, she hadn't been able to be alone in the place where it had all happened. So she'd escaped to their beach house in Gordons Bay for a few months, before Greg had asked her to move in with him. But the divorce meant that she no longer had any right to stay there, and since she had been renting before they'd got married the only thing she had was the house she'd lived in with Jordan. It was in *her* name after all.

But what did that matter when she couldn't bring herself to *think* about what had happened there, let alone *live* there and having to face the memories over and over again...?

'That wasn't what I meant,' he said.

Sure that she had got to all the pieces of glass that could be picked up by hand, she stood. 'Not the *only* thing, maybe.'

She wondered how she could speak so coolly when her insides were twisted. But then, she was used to saying things despite her feelings. How many times had she bitten her tongue or said the thing people wanted to hear instead of saying what she really thought? The only difference now was that she was actually being honest.

'Fine.' The word was delivered through clenched teeth. 'There is something else. Did you put him up to the ridiculous conditions of his will?'

Anger whipped through her, and she barely noticed her hand tighten on the dustpan.

'No, Jordan, I didn't. I don't want to own a

house with you, and I don't want to plan an event with you.'

I just want to move on with my life.

He didn't say anything immediately. 'I don't want that either.'

'But we'll have to.'

'Because you want your half of the house, the vineyard?'

'Because if we don't you'll lose your half of both, too.'

He didn't deny her words, though she knew by the way his face tightened that he wanted to. It wasn't so much at the truth of what she said, but at the fact that it *was* the truth. How could Jordan explain the fact that his father had left his house—and his share of the vineyard—to *both* his son and ex-daughter-in-law? For someone who valued logic as much as Jordan did, having no explanation for something this important must be eating at him.

'I'm going to contest the will.'

The part of herself that Mila had felt softening immediately iced.

'Based on what?'

'On anything I can find. I won't just accept this.'

And yet you just accepted it when I told you to give me space.

'And if I *don't* succeed in contesting the will… will you…will you sell your shares to me without any of the conditions?'

Pain sat on her chest at the question—the one she knew he'd wanted to ask since he had arrived—and forced words from her lips. 'Yes, Jordan. If that's possible, and if that's what you want, I'll do it.'

Unspoken words filled the air—memories of when he had said much the same thing to her at the end of their marriage—and she closed her eyes against them. When she was sure her emotions were in check—when she was sure that she was strong enough to look at him—she did.

And realised how different he was from the man she'd known…and loved.

She hadn't noticed any of it when she'd seen him four months ago at his father's funeral. He hadn't looked at her then, she thought, too consumed by the grief of losing his only surviving parent—the man who had raised him—despite their complicated relationship. Or maybe because of it. She wasn't even sure he knew she had only gone to the church and graveyard, not being able to bear spending time socialising after the death of the only man she'd ever thought of as a father.

After losing the last of the family she had.

Suddenly she felt incredibly weary.

'I think it's best if I go to bed now,' she said, as the shock of seeing him finally caught up with her.

'Wait,' he said, and took her arm before she could walk out of the room.

She looked down at his hand as heat seared through her body at his touch, and quickly moved away. She didn't want to think about the physical effect he had on her. The emotional one was already too much.

He cleared his throat. 'I've arranged for a meeting with Mark Garrett in the morning. To see if I have grounds to contest. Since you're willing to sell, I was hoping you would come with me.'

Her eyebrows rose. 'You've made an appointment with your family lawyer? The executor of your father's will?' When he nodded, she said,

'And you're only telling me this now? When it's beneficial to you?'

He looked at her, those golden eyes carefully blank of emotion. 'I didn't think you needed to be there.'

'Because my inheritance doesn't concern me, right? No, it's fine. I get it.' She shook her head when he opened his mouth to respond. 'You've been making decisions for the both of us since we got married. Why stop now that we're divorced?'

She didn't wait for a response, but walked past him, hating the way her body longed to be held in his arms.

Hating the way her life was once again in turmoil because of Jordan Thomas.

Mila got up at five in the morning, her muscles hard with tension after a restless night. She got dressed and did the thing that always helped to keep her mind busy—she cooked. First she made a batch of scones and then muffins and pancakes. When that was done she scrambled eggs, made bacon and toast, and eventually, as the sun peeked through the kitchen windows, put on the kettle for coffee.

'What's all this?'

The deep voice startled her, even though she knew he was there. She supposed she had already grown so used to being alone in the months since Greg had been gone—her heart ached at the reminder—that anyone's presence, let alone that of the man who unsettled her most in the world, would have frightened her in the quiet of the morning.

'Food,' she said, and wiped her hands on her apron. She stilled, thinking that it made her look nervous. 'I'm going to take it down to Frank and Martha's.'

Frank was the kind-hearted man who'd helped manage the vineyard after Greg had taken ill and Jordan had moved away. She had a soft spot for him and, since cooking was something she did to keep herself calm, often took food to Frank and his wife, Martha's house on the Thomas property to share with the workers at the vineyard during the day.

Though now Mila supposed she should offer some to Jordan. Except that would make it seem as if she had got up that morning specifically to cook for *him*. Just as she had when they were married. So she wouldn't offer him breakfast, but would wait until later to pack up the food and let him get breakfast for himself.

Satisfied with the decision, she asked, 'What time is the appointment?'

To avoid his gaze, she turned to make herself coffee. But she stopped when she realised she was about to take out *two* mugs, her mind already making his as he liked it. So she turned back to him and folded her arms, ignoring the way the sight of his hair, wet from a shower, made her body prickle.

'Eight thirty.'

'In less than an hour,' she confirmed, proud of the fact that her voice wasn't as shaky as she felt. 'I'll go and get ready.'

She nearly ran out of the kitchen, but acting normally was eating at her strength. The last time she had been in that kitchen with Jordan she had been pregnant and happy, with the only true family she'd known—her husband and her father-in-law—around her.

The loss of it all was a physical pain.

She bided her time so that she didn't have to have breakfast with him, only coming out when they had to leave. Her eyebrows barely lifted at his choice of transportation—a sleek blue car she knew was a recent and expensive model—but her heart thawed when he opened the door for her.

The trip was silent and tense, but she consoled herself by repeating that it would be over soon. If she signed her share of the vineyard, of the house, over to Jordan she would be able to move out and move on. It would mark the end of the worst and best years of her life and, though her heart was nostalgic for the best, the worst was enough that if she could, she would sign the papers right there in the car.

When Jordan gave his name to the receptionist at the lawyer's, they were shown into an office where Mila spent another ten minutes of tension with Jordan while waiting for the lawyer to come.

'Good morning, Jordan... Mila.'

Mark spoke softly to her and she gave him a small smile. She had only met him twice—once when she'd signed a prenuptial contract, and again after Greg's death when Mark had come to give his condolences and to drop off her copy of the will. Both times he had been kind, and she'd appreciated that.

Jordan barely waited until Mark was seated before he asked, 'What was going on in my father's head when he made this will, Mark?'

Mark gave him a wry smile. 'I think you would be a better judge of that than me.'

When Jordan didn't return the smile, Mark nodded, apparently realising Jordan was only in the mood for business.

'Well, you've both read Greg's will by now. It's actually quite simple in its conditions—which I know you both must find hard to believe, considering what it's asking of you. You already own half of the Thomas Vineyard, Jordan, having inherited your mother's share of the property when you were twenty-one. Greg's half has been left, as he states in his will, to his son and his daughter-in-law, on the condition that you both work together to plan an...'

Mark paused and took a closer look at the will.

'An Under the Stars event. Instructions have been left regarding the nature of the event— which, again, both of you will have read—and this event has to take place no later than two months after the last of you received a copy of the will.'

'I received mine two weeks ago,' Jordan interrupted, looking at Mila for confirmation of her date.

'I probably got mine a week before that,' she said, and wished her heart wouldn't beat quite as hard.

'Which would mean that we have just over a month to plan this. *If* we do,' Jordan said, his voice masking all emotion.

'Honestly, Jordan. I don't see you having a choice if you want to keep the vineyard solely in your family. If you don't plan the event, your father's share of the vineyard will be auctioned off and the proceeds will be divided between the both of you.'

'Excuse me, Mark?' Mila said, ignoring the way her stomach jolted as Jordan's eyes zoned in on her. 'The will says that I've been left half of Greg's portion as his "daughter-in-law," right?' When Mark nodded his head, she continued. 'So, since Jordan and I aren't married any more, won't that give Jordan grounds to contest the will?'

And leave me out of it?

Mark's eyebrows rose. 'When did you get divorced?'

'About a year ago.' Jordan spoke now, and his eyes were hopeful when Mila lifted her own to look at his face.

She knew that she shouldn't take it personally—if Greg's will could be contested they would both get what they wanted—but her heart still contracted.

She diverted her attention to Mark, saw him riffling through the papers in front of him, and felt concern grow when he lifted one page, his face serious.

'Is there a problem?' she asked.

'I'm afraid so.' Mark looked at them both and laid the page back down. 'Before we send the beneficiaries copies of a will, we check all the details we can for accuracy. Your marital status was one of them and, well...' He gave them both an apologetic look. 'According to the court records of South Africa, the two of you are still very much married.'

CHAPTER TWO

THE SILENCE THAT stretched through the room was marred only by their breathing.

Jordan tried to use it to compose himself, to control the emotions that hearing he was supposedly still married had drawn from him. But then, how could he compose himself when he knew there had to be some mistake?

'I could check again,' Mark said, when Jordan told him as much, 'but I'm afraid the chances of there being a mistake are quite slim.'

'But I signed the papers.' Jordan turned to Mila. 'You did, too.'

Her eyes, slightly glazed from the shock, looked back at him from a pale face as she nodded her agreement. He fought against his instinct to hold her, to tell her that everything would be okay. It wasn't his job any more. Unless, he realised as his mind shifted to their current situation, it *was*.

'With which law firm did you file the papers?

I can have my assistant call them to ask them about it.'

'With *this* law firm,' Jordan said, his voice calm though his insides were in a twist.

Mark frowned. 'Do you know which lawyer?'

'With *you*, Mark. As you're my family lawyer, I filed the papers with you.'

His patience was wearing thin. All he'd wanted when he'd come back was to sort out his inheritance. Once that bit of unpleasantness was done, he would be able to run his family vineyard.

It was the only way he knew to make up for the fact that he'd left without dealing with any of the unresolved issues with his father. To make it up to his mother, too, he thought, remembering the only thing she had asked of him before she'd died when he was five—that he look after his father.

He forced his thoughts away from how he had failed them both.

'I think there's been a mistake of some kind.' To give him credit, Mark was trying incredibly hard to maintain his professionalism. 'I remember you asked me to draw up divorce papers. But when I met your father to set up his will last year he said that the two of you were choosing to separate—not divorce.'

'Wait—Greg set this will up *last year*?' Mila's voice was surprisingly strong despite the lack of colour in her face. 'When exactly did he do it?'

'August.'

'That was a month after his first heart attack. And two months after I signed the divorce papers.'

'Did they have my signature on them?' Jordan asked, wondering where she was going with this.

'Yes, they did.'

'So you would have been the one to file the papers with Mark?'

If Jordan hadn't seen her looking worse than this once before—the day of her fall—he would have worried about how muted she had become.

'I didn't feel entirely comfortable with that...'

Something in her eyes made him wonder what she meant, but he decided now wasn't the right time to think about it. Not when he saw that she was struggling to keep her voice devoid of the emotion she couldn't hide from him.

'So we are still married,' he said flatly.

'No, no—I was going to drop them here after

I'd signed, but then Greg asked me whether I would feel better if *he* did it. Because Mark was *your* family lawyer,' she said quickly, avoiding his eyes—which told him she was lying.

It only took him a moment to realise that she was lying about the reason she'd let Greg take the papers, not about his father's actions.

'Did you follow up with Dad?' he demanded, his anger coating his real feelings about the fact that his father had been there for Mila when he hadn't been. Or the fact that his father had been supportive at all—especially to someone who wasn't his son. Was it just another way Greg had chosen to show Jordan how wrong his choice to leave had been?

'Did *you*?' she shot back, and Jordan stared at her, wondering again where the fire was coming from.

'No, clearly not.'

There was a pause.

'I think that, all things considered, we should probably postpone this meeting until a later point,' Mark said, breaking the silence.

'I don't think that's a good idea with the time frame we're working with, Mark.'

Though denial was a tempting option, Jordan knew that he had to face reality. And it seemed the reality was that he was still married.

'Could you please give us a few moments to talk in private?'

'Yes, of course.'

If he was perturbed by being kicked out of his own office, Mark didn't show it as he left the room.

The minute the door clicked closed, Jordan spoke. 'So, my father was supposed to give the papers to Mark, who was supposed to file them. And since none of that happened, I think Mark's right—we are still married.'

'Yes, I think so...'

Her eyes were closed, but Jordan knew it was one of the ways she worked through her feelings. Closing herself off from the world—and in those last months they'd shared together closing herself off from *him*—so she could think.

The silence stretched out long enough that he became aware of a niggling inside his heart. One that told him that there was still hope for them if they were married. He didn't like it at all—not when that hope had already been dashed when Mila had accepted the divorce.

He had filed for divorce because he'd thought that it was what she wanted—she hadn't called, hadn't spoken to him once after he'd walked out through the door to a life in Johannesburg. He'd taken it as a sign that she wanted the space she had asked him for to be permanent. And so he'd thought he would make it easier for the both of them by initiating the divorce, half expecting her to call him, to demand that he come home so that they could fix things.

But he'd realised soon enough that that wasn't going to happen—when had she demanded any-thing from him anyway?—and he'd figured that he had done the right thing. Especially since *he* had been the one to make the decision that had caused the heartbreak they'd suffered in the first place.

'Your father spoke to me about a reunion be-tween the two of us.'

He turned his head to her when she spoke. Her voice held that same music he had heard the first time they'd met.

'In his last few months. He wanted us to be together again.'

She opened her eyes, and Jordan had to brace himself against what the pain he saw there did to him. Against the anguish that disappointment was the last thing his father had felt about him.

He cleared his throat. 'I suppose that gives this situation some meaning. He wanted us to plan an event like the one where we met. He knew that still being married would mean we would have to bend to his will. Unless we can show that he was unfit when he made it.'

'I don't think that will work.'

She shook her head, and he wondered why she kept tying her hair up when those curls were meant to be free.

'He was completely sane—his heart attacks had nothing to do with his ability to make rational decisions.'

'What's rational about *this*?'

She lowered her eyes. 'Nothing. Of course, nothing. But making an emotional decision isn't against the law.'

'It should be.'

'Maybe.' She looked at him stoically. 'But he

isn't the first person to do that in this family, so I think we can forgive him.'

Jordan found himself at a loss for words, unsure of what she meant. Was she talking about when she'd asked him to go, or the fact that he had left? Regardless of their meaning, her words surprised him. She hadn't given him any indication that she regretted what had happened between them... But then again, she wasn't exactly saying that now either.

But still, the feeling threw him. And because he didn't like it, he addressed the situation at hand.

'It doesn't seem like we're going to get out of this before our time is up, Mila.'

'Out of this...? You mean out of our marriage?'

Why did the question make him feel so strange?

He cleared his throat. 'Yes. The divorce—the one we thought we had—was supposed to take six weeks, and that's as much time as we have to make sure the will's terms are met. So...' he took a deep breath '...what would you say about putting the divorce off until we've planned the event, and then we can take it from there?'

She briefly closed her eyes again, and then

looked at him, her expression guarded. 'Why would I do that?'

'What do you mean?'

'Exactly what I said.'

Her guard had slipped enough for him to see a complexity of emotion that reflected the complexity of their predicament.

'I lose in this situation either way. If I help you, we'll get the inheritance, sure, but I would still have to sell my share to you. So what do I get out of this besides spending time with the man I thought I would never have to see again?'

It took him a moment to process what she was saying, and even then he found it difficult to formulate an answer. 'You'll get money. I'll pay you for the share of the vineyard my father left you.'

'Money? *Money?*' She pulled her head back as though she had been slapped. 'I can't believe that we're still married.'

Her words felt like a slap to him, too, but the shame that ran through him at his own words made him realise that maybe he'd deserved it. He was surprised that she had said it—she would never have done so before—but that didn't make it any less true.

'I'm sorry, Mila, I didn't mean that.' He sighed. 'This has been a shock to me, too.'

She nodded, though the coldness coming from her made him wonder if she really did accept his apology.

'You know money isn't an incentive for me,' she said after a few moments, her voice back to being neutral. 'Especially since selling you my share of the vineyard would mean that I lose the only thing I have left of someone I thought of as family.'

His heart ached at that because he understood it. But the logical side of him—the side that didn't care too much for emotions—made him ask, 'If you didn't want to sell your share of the vineyard to me, why did you say you would?'

'I didn't say I wouldn't sell. I just want you to understand what I'm giving up so that you won't say something so insensitive again.'

He was beginning to feel like a schoolchild who was being taught a lesson. 'What *do* you want, then, Mila?'

'I want—' Her voice was husky, her face twisted in pain. But it disappeared almost as quickly as it came, and she cleared her throat. 'I want to sell the house and the car—everything, really, that was a part of our life together.'

Pain flared through him, and the only way he knew how to control it was to pretend it didn't affect him at all. 'Why?'

'To get rid of everything so that I can move—' She broke off, and then continued, 'Move away.' She said the last two words deliberately, as though she was struggling to formulate them. 'I haven't been able to sort things out since you left. The past year I've been busy. Looking after Greg, planning some events and...'

Getting over you, he thought she might say, and he held his breath, waiting for the words. But they didn't come.

'Your help would be useful so that by the time the vineyard is yours, I'll have something to move on to.'

'Where will you go?' he asked when it finally registered that she wanted to move away.

She raised her eyes to his, and they brimmed with the emotion he thought he carried in his heart.

'I'm still working on that part.'

Hearing her say that she was leaving was more

difficult than he could have imagined. He couldn't figure out why that was when he had done the same thing.

'Are you sure you're not sacrificing more than I am?'

She smiled a little at that. 'I'm sure.'

Her smile told him all he needed to know. That he needed to help her so he could help himself. Once this was all over he would have the vineyard his parents had owned and would be able to live up to the promises he'd made to them. Maybe he would even be able to make restitution for the decisions he'd made during his short marriage and finally find some peace.

'So if I agree to help you deal with everything from when we were married, you'll agree to plan the event and then sell your inheritance to me?'

'Yes.'

'And then we'll file for divorce again?'

'We?'

The hope he thought he'd extinguished earlier threatened to ignite again at the uncertainty in her voice. But then he remembered that *he* was the one who had filed for divorce the first time, and she was probably just checking whether that would be the case again.

'You,' he clarified. 'We might as well even the score since we have the chance.'

He could have kicked himself when he saw the way her eyes darkened. He wasn't entirely sure he blamed her since his words seemed callous even to his own ears. But despite that, she nodded.

'I guess we have a deal.'

CHAPTER THREE

THEY DROVE BACK to the house in silence.

Jordan's presence was already turning Mila's life upside down. He reminded her of the things she'd failed at. Of the things she had wanted since she'd realised as a child that she didn't have a family in the way her classmates did.

Her entire class had once been invited to a party and she had begged her foster mother at the time—a perpetually exhausted woman who'd spent all her time catering to her husband instead of the children she'd been charged with caring for—to let her go.

When she'd got there Mila had seen for the first time what a real family was. She'd seen her classmate's parents look at their child with love, with pride. Had watched them take photos together while the rest of her class played on the grass. Had seen the easy affection.

She had spent that entire afternoon watching

them, wondering why no one else was when this family was clearly doing something out of the norm. But when Mila had been the last to be picked up, she'd seen the way the other parents had treated their children. She'd realised that *that* was normal, and that *she* was the one with the special circumstances.

Her longing for family had started on that day, spreading through her heart, reminding her of it with every beat. Since she had lost her child, those beats had become heavy with pain, with emptiness. And it would only be worse now that Jordan was back.

Since he was back for good, she would have to leave the house she'd been staying in for almost a year. Though she'd known she couldn't stay there for ever, she *had* hoped for more time than she'd got. Not only because she didn't know where she would go—again, the thought of returning to the house where she'd lost their baby made her feel nauseous—but because it had come to feel like the home she'd never had. But then, Mila had also hoped for more time with Greg—especially since she'd finally managed to pierce that closed-off exterior of his...

But that was the least of her concerns now that she'd found out she and Jordan were still married.

It was the hope that worried her the most. Hope had been her first emotion when she'd heard the news, and it had lingered until Jordan had brought up filing for divorce again. It reminded her of how receiving those papers for the first time had destroyed her hope for reconciliation. And rightly so. She shouldn't be—wasn't—interested in reconciliation, however easy it might be to get lured back into the promise of a life with Jordan.

But that wasn't what he wanted, or he wouldn't have left so easily. And that, she told herself, was exactly why she needed to protect herself from him. That was why she had accepted Jordan's suggestion that *she* be the one to file the divorce papers this time. She needed to remind herself that their life together—at least in a romantic sense—was over.

She didn't want him to know how difficult things had been for her since he'd left, even though she had almost told him about it in Mark's office. About how selling their possessions had nothing to do with moving away and everything to do with moving on. But because she couldn't bear to expose herself to him she'd lied instead. Though now that she thought about it perhaps moving away *was* the first step to moving on...

Either way, she needed his help. She couldn't go back to their house—she would never think of it as hers, even if it was in her name—alone. She couldn't face it by herself. And she *had* to face it. She had spent long enough grieving for the family she was sure she would never have now. She knew the loss of her son would stay with her for ever, but she was determined to make something out of her life. To prove that she would have been a worthy mother...

'Do you want to talk about how everything will work?' Jordan asked, almost as though he knew that she'd been thinking too much and wanted to distract her.

'You mean how we'll plan the event?' she asked, and looked out of the window to the vineyards they were passing.

Stellenbosch had always felt like home to her, even when she hadn't had a home. The minute she had driven down the winding road that offered the most beautiful sights she had ever seen—the peaks that stood above fields and fields of produce, the kaleidoscope of colours that changed with every season—a piece had settled inside her. That had been the first time she had visited the Thomas Vineyard.

'That's part of it, of course. But I was speaking about all the details. Like where you're going to stay, for example.'

She sighed. She had told him that she would leave Greg's house that morning, and when she'd said it she'd thought it was the best way to force herself to face going back to their house. But her deal with Jordan meant that she could delay that a little longer, and immediately the ball in her chest unravelled.

Though that didn't mean she could stay at the farmhouse.

'I can still leave today.'

She could stay at a bed and breakfast, she thought, forcing herself to ignore the pain in her chest. She didn't need to be thinking about how leaving would sacrifice her only connection to Greg—to the memories of family and the love she'd never thought she deserved. She also didn't need to remember that she'd spent little time working since the accident, which meant her bank account was in a sorry state.

'You don't have to,' he said stiffly, and she turned to him.

'What do you mean?'

'It might make more sense for us to stay together.' Jordan's eyes were fixed on the road. 'We have six weeks to sort this event out. Being in the same space will make it a lot easier.'

There was Mr Logical again, she thought, and unexplained disappointment made her say, 'I can't stay in the house with you there, Jordan.'

She saw him frown. 'Why not?'

Because there's too big a part of me that wants to play house with you again, she realised.

'It's too complicated. This whole thing with us still being married…' Her head pounded at the knowledge and what it meant. 'It's a lot to deal with. It would probably be best if you and I lived separately.'

He didn't respond as he turned onto the gravel road that led to the house that would soon be theirs. She used the time to remind herself that she had been at a standstill for a year. She couldn't keep letting the tragedies in her life *or* her dreams for a family hold her back. It was time to move on, and living with Jordan—even if it *was* practical, considering her current financial situation—didn't seem to be the way she would do it.

But then she thought about the deal she had made with Jordan—about how he was going to help her sell all the things from their marriage if she helped him—and she began to wonder if living together and planning the event *was* the way she was going to move on.

As though he knew her thoughts, Jordan repeated, 'I think you should stay. We're planning an event that will happen in the next six weeks. We need to get your house and your car sold—things that might take a lot longer than six weeks—but we can start now. And we can definitely get everything in the house sold before then.'

Which should help her financial problems, she thought.

'Handling all of it will be a lot easier if we could do it from the same place,' he said again.

It made sense, she thought, but cautioned herself not to make a hasty decision.

'I'll think about it,' she said, even though the rational part of her told her she should say no. 'But I'll stay here until I've made a decision.'

'Okay,' he responded politely, and though she didn't look at him, she frowned at his acquiescence.

The Jordan she knew would have pushed or, worse, would have made the decision for her. Was he giving her space just so he'd get what he wanted? Or was it genuine? She couldn't decide, but he had pulled up in front of the house now, and her attention was drawn to the raindrops that had begun to fall lightly on the windshield.

They made a run for the front door.

'Where you'll be staying isn't the only thing we should talk about,' he said, once they were inside the house.

Mila turned to him when she'd taken off her coat. The light drizzle had sprinkled rain through his hair, and her fingers itched to dust the glittering droplets away.

Another reason I should stay away from you.

'Yes, I know.'

She moved to the living room and started putting wood in the fireplace. It had become a routine—a ritual, almost—and it comforted her. Perhaps because it was so wonderfully normal— so far from what she'd grown up with. 'We need to talk about the event—about how we're going to plan something I did in six months in just over one.'

She saw a flicker in his eyes that suggested that wasn't what he was talking about. She supposed she had known that on some level. Which was why she had steered the conversation to safer ground. To protect herself. Now she just had to remember that for the entire time they spent together...

'Is it possible?' Jordan asked, watching Mila carefully. Something about her was different, and it wasn't only her appearance. Though as she sat curled on the couch opposite him—to be as far away from him as she could, he thought—the cup of tea she had left the room to make a few moments before in her hand, he could see that the old Mila was still there.

His heart throbbed as though it had been knocked, and he found himself yearning for something that belonged in the past. His present—*their* present—involved planning an event to save his family's vineyard. And his family no longer included the woman he had fallen so hard for, despite every logical part of him...no matter what his heart said.

'It's going to be difficult,' she conceded, distracting him from his thoughts.

'What do you think we should start with?' he asked, deciding that the only way he could focus on their business arrangement was by talking about business. But then she shifted, and the vanilla scent that clung to her drifted over to him. Suddenly he thought about how much he had missed it. About how often he'd thought he'd smelled it—had felt his heart racing at the thought that she'd come to find him—only to realise that it had been in his imagination...

'Well, the conditions of your father's will stipulate that we try to replicate the original Under the Stars event as much as possible. But, considering the season...' she looked out at the dreary weather '...I'm not sure how successful that will be.'

As she spoke she ran a finger around the rim of her cup. It was a habit for her—one she reverted to when she was deep in thought. Once, when he'd teased her about it, she'd told him that one of her foster mothers had hated it when she'd done it. The woman had told her that she was inviting bacteria, and that Mila shouldn't think they would take her to the doctor if she got sick.

It was one of the rare pieces of information she had offered him about her childhood, and she had meant for him to be amused by it. But instead it had alerted him to the difficulty of her past. Since he knew how that felt, he had never pushed her for more information.

'I don't think he thought this through,' he said, to stop his thoughts from dwelling further, but only succeeding in shifting them to his father.

'No, I don't think so either,' she agreed. 'He meant well, but in his head this idea was romanticised. We would do an event together, just like the one where we met, and it would remind us of how we felt that first night.'

The dreamy look on her face made his heart accelerate, and for the first time Jordan wondered if his father had been right. But nostalgia wasn't enough to save a broken relationship.

'And then he'd have facilitated our reunion

through his death,' she ended, the expression he'd seen only moments before replaced by sadness.

His heart ached. 'He always said he wanted his death to mean something.'

'Especially after your mother's,' she said softy.

His eyes lifted to hers, and the sympathy he saw there stiffened his spine. 'Maybe.'

He didn't speak about his mother's death. He had been five when it had happened and he had spent most of his life till then watching her suffer. Because she hadn't done anything about her cancer soon enough. Because she had chosen *him*.

The memory made him think about whether his father *had* designed his will as a punishment for Jordan. To get justice, perhaps, for the fact that Greg had always blamed Jordan for her death. Something Jordan had only found out years after his mother had passed away. It would be the perfect way for his father to make his death 'mean something,' Jordan thought, especially since Greg had made his will *after* Jordan had left to cope with the loss of his son, of his wife. It was something he knew Greg hadn't approved of, despite the fact that although Greg had been there physically, in all the ways that had mattered, Greg had done the same after Jordan's mother had died...

Jordan lifted his eyes and saw that Mila was watching him in that way she had that always made him think she saw through him. He only relaxed when she averted her gaze.

'We have six weeks to do this—which means that the event is going to happen in winter. And this rain suggests that the weather has already made a turn for the worst.'

He was grateful for the change in subject. 'It also means that the grounds in the amphitheatre won't be suitable for the public.'

'Actually, I don't think that will be a problem. When your father got sick, he couldn't take care of the vineyard as well as he'd used to. So we minimised operations. We closed up the amphitheatre since we wouldn't be using it, and concentrated our efforts on the wine.'

'How did you do that? The area is huge.'

She shrugged. 'I had a connection with a tent and marquee supplier, and he designed one for us. I'll take you to see it tomorrow, if you like...' She trailed off. 'You know, I could probably get him to customise the design so that the top of the marquee is clear. That way the event would still be in the amphitheatre—'

'And still be under the stars,' he finished for her.

'Why do you look so surprised?'

'I'm just...' He was just *what*? Surprised to see her throw herself into a task like this when he couldn't remember the last time she had shown interest in anything?

'I'm good at my job, Jordan,' she said flatly when he didn't continue.

'I wasn't saying that you weren't,' he replied.

The look she shot him burned through him, and he found himself bristling in response. It simmered when he saw a slight flicker in her eyes that made her look almost vulnerable, and he wondered why he couldn't tell what had caused her reaction. He should know her well enough to be able to... Except he didn't, he realised in shock.

'I'll draw up a list of everything that needs to be done and give you a copy once I have,' she said tightly as she stood, and Jordan could see that tension straightened her spine. 'We can discuss things then.'

She walked to the door and grabbed her coat.

'Where are you going?' he demanded, anger replacing the shock of only a moment ago.

'Out,' she replied, and slammed the door on her way out, leaving him speechless.

The woman who had walked out through that door—who had got angry at nothing and left before they could deal with it—was *not* the woman he had married. *Or was she?* a voice mocked him, and briefly he wondered if he was angry at Mila for seemingly acting out of character, or at himself for not knowing his wife well enough to be able to tell.

The thought spurred his feet forward, and he was out the door before she could get far.

'Mila! Mila, wait!'

Her steps faltered, but she didn't turn back. He stopped with enough distance between them that she wouldn't feel crowded, but so she could still hear him.

'Why are you upset?'

She turned and pulled her coat tight around her, determination lining her features. 'I didn't like that you looked surprised about me being good at my job.'

It took him a moment to process her words—especially since he was surprised that she had actually chosen to answer him.

'I wasn't surprised that you're good at your job. I *know* you are.' He watched her, hoping for some indication that she believed his words, but her face was carefully blank. 'You took the spark of an idea I had with the first Under the Stars event and turned it into something I'd never dreamed of. *And* you made it a success. Of course you're good at your job.'

'I *did* do all of that,' she said after a moment. 'I *am* good at my job.'

'Yes, you are,' he reiterated, and thought about the vulnerability he'd thought he'd seen in her eyes earlier. 'But are you trying to convince me of that, or yourself?'

She folded her arms in front of her—but not before he saw her wince. She *was* trying to convince herself, he thought, and wondered how she could even doubt it.

'Don't pretend like you know me.'

Because he was suddenly worried that it was true and he *didn't* know her, anger stirred inside him again. 'It goes both ways, Mila.'

'What?'

'You assumed that I thought poorly of you because of one look you misinterpreted. If you knew who *I* was, then you would have known that couldn't be true.'

'Then tell me the real reason for your surprise.'

Her arms fell to her sides and he watched her straighten her shoulders. As if she was preparing for battle, he thought. But he couldn't answer her question. It would open the door that both of them seemed happy to keep closed—the one that protected them from their past.

When he didn't respond, she shook her head. 'That's what I thought.' She sighed. 'You know, maybe I jumped to the conclusion that you thought I wasn't good at my job because you never told me that I was. But then, we didn't have that kind of relationship, did we?'

She walked away, leaving him wondering what kind of relationship they *had* had.

CHAPTER FOUR

MILA WALKED DOWN the gravel road to the amphitheatre, Jordan beside her, and some of her tension eased. It was home, she thought as she looked at the road shaded by trees, their leaves brown and gold as though they didn't know whether to mourn or celebrate the coming winter. The grass around them had begun to lose its colour, too, though there were still patches that seemed to be fighting to remain as green as in spring.

When she made it through the trees she was standing at the top of a slope that led to the vineyard on the one side, and to the amphitheatre on the other. She had sombrely told Jordan that she would take him there that morning, and thought she needed to get over herself. She'd spent most of her time since their argument thinking about why she'd been upset—the *real* reason, not the one she had made up.

Because as soon as she'd given herself time to think it through—with Jordan's words still in her head—she'd realised her reaction the previous day *had* been because *she* was doubting her skills. It wasn't just about her job either. Jordan's return had reminded her of her failures—at being a wife. At being a mother.

Her heart hiccupped and she laid a hand over her chest, hoping to comfort herself.

Losing her baby when she was barely six months pregnant had only succeeded in amplifying her insecurities. Insecurities that stemmed from growing up without hearing anyone tell her she was good at something—at anything. She could see now that it had led to her believing that she wasn't good *enough*. Certainly not for Jordan when she'd first met him, since he'd had everything she hadn't had in her childhood.

Love, a family, a home.

A little voice had reminded her of that throughout their marriage. It was part of the reason she wished Jordan had told her he was happy with her. Or that he was proud of her. Or that she was a good wife.

But then, they'd never shared things like that

during their brief marriage. She had just accepted what he'd said because she'd been afraid to speak up in case it upset him. She hadn't wanted to risk him realising that their relationship was too good to be true. That she wasn't the right person for him.

Now she saw no point in keeping her thoughts to herself—he'd realised all that anyway. And perhaps that had been the reason for Jordan's surprise—she was no longer meek Mila who didn't speak her mind. What had that got her? Nothing but a heart broken by the loss of her husband and her child.

'Nothing beats this view,' Jordan said quietly from beside her, and her heart pounded when she turned and saw him looking at her. But then he nodded towards the vineyard, and she mentally kicked herself. *Of course* he wasn't talking about her—especially since things between them were still tense.

She turned her attention to the vineyard to hide her embarrassment at thinking such a silly thing, and took in the clash of different shades of red and brown. Fields of the colours together was a picture she would never forget—even when it was years in the future and she no longer had any reason to be a part of the Thomas Vineyard. She could see the dam just beyond the fields, large and beautiful, and behind it the hills that made the vineyard look surreal.

Walking the vineyard with him felt like old times. Despite how difficult things were with them now, when they had walked past the chapel where they'd got married, Mila's heart had longed for the people they'd been then. It didn't help that the weather had turned from the rain of the previous day to bright sunshine. It reminded her of her wedding day, almost two years ago.

It had been cold, true to the season, but the sun had been shining just as it was today, as though the gods had approved their union. A fanciful thought, she realised now, indicative of the person she had been then. The person who had fallen in love at first sight and married three months later.

The fact that their wedding anniversary was a few weeks away pained her, and she tried to ignore it. Her mind reminded her that she and Jordan hadn't been together long enough—physically or emotionally—for them to celebrate their *first* anniversary. Now, on their second, they'd be together physically, but emotionally...

'It's more beautiful than I remember,' he said, and she almost smiled at the sincerity in his voice.

'It's become a bit like home to me in the past year,' she murmured, deep in thought, and then her stomach dropped when she realised what she had said. 'Because of Greg,' she added hurriedly, hoping it would make her words seem less like a revelation.

He didn't answer her, and when she looked over he had a blank expression on his face. How was it possible that the tension between them could become worse? she wondered, her insides twisting.

'I have memories of every part of this place,' he said, his face pensive now. 'This is where I last saw my mother. This is where my father raised me.'

Mila frowned. Had he just willingly mentioned his mother? His reaction the previous night when she'd said something about her had been what Mila was used to. A quick brush-off, an unwillingness to respond. She had wanted to know about his mother so badly when they were dating, when they were married, but she'd never had the nerve to push beyond Jordan's resistance. Since she didn't really want to offer information to him either, she'd convinced herself that it didn't matter. That one day, while they watched their children play in front of the house, he would tell her about the woman who had died when he was five, and she would hold his hand and tell him that it was okay.

But that day would never come now.

Jordan turned towards the amphitheatre and she followed him, and then she stopped, her eyes widening when she realised what going to the amphitheatre meant. Why hadn't she realised this earlier, she thought in panic, when she could have done something about it? *Before* she had suggested it, for heaven's sake!

'Are you coming?' Jordan asked her, and she exhaled shakily, forced her legs to move and her mouth to respond.

'Yes…yes, I am.'

'This is great,' Jordan said when he saw the white marquee that covered the amphitheatre. The edges were pinned down between the trees that surrounded the area, and it had done its job for the most part, he noted. Though water ran down the steps, the seats and the stage were still dry, along with most of the ground. It would do for their event, he thought.

'Whose idea was it to do this? It was smart.'

He took the steps as he asked the question, and was about halfway down when he realised Mila hadn't answered him. Nor could he hear her following. When he turned back to look up at her his heart raced at her expression. Her face was white—and so was the hand that clung to the railing that ran down the middle of the stairs. He could see her chest heave—in, out…in, out—and his first instinct was to run to her side and make sure that she was okay.

But somewhere at the back of his mind he realised what was happening, and a picture of her at the bottom of the stairs at their old house, lying deadly still, flashed through his mind.

This is what you left behind, a voice told him, and a ball of grief and guilt drop in his stomach.

Careful to keep his expression blank, even as his heart thrummed, he walked up to her and slid an arm around her waist. She didn't look at him, and he could feel her resistance, so he waited until her hand finally gripped the back of his jacket. Slowly they made their way down to the bottom of the stairs, and with each step the ball of emotion grew inside him.

'Thank you,' she said through tight lips when they got to the bottom, but he could hear the shakiness in her voice—felt it in her body before she stepped back from him.

'Since the accident?' he asked.

She lifted her eyes briefly, and then lowered them again as she straightened her shoulders. 'Yeah. It's not impossible to do. It just takes longer.'

He didn't know what to say. How could he say anything at all? he wondered with disgust. He knew the loss of their son had hurt them both—Jordan lived with it every day, no matter where he was. Every moment of his life since that day still held glimpses of what it would have been like if his son had been alive—images of them as a family in the home where he and Mila used to live crushed his heart each time.

But the reality was that he *wasn't* a father. And, yes, he had complicated emotions about it—dashed hopes, a broken heart—but his body was fine. Though his heart pained, he could go down a flight of stairs without thinking about the fall that had led to a placental abruption and a premature baby who couldn't survive outside the womb. *His* mind, though still dimmed by grief, wasn't addled by a fear of stairs.

Seeing Mila's reality, seeing the effect losing their baby had had on her, gutted him. The shame and guilt he already felt about the loss of their child pierced him. And the anger—the tension Jordan felt at the fact that Mila hadn't turned to him—flamed inside him.

'Why didn't you tell me?'

She slanted a look at him. 'About...?'

She was giving him a chance to back down, he thought briefly, but he wouldn't do it.

'About the stairs. Is there anything else you're still struggling with?'

'That isn't your business any more, Jordan,' she replied easily, though he could tell that the conversation was anything but easy for her.

'You're my *wife*, Mila.' It didn't matter to him that they had both signed divorce papers and had only found out they were still married the previous day. 'I have a right to know.'

'No, you don't,' she said tersely. 'You gave up that right when you walked out. When you sent me divorce papers. When you didn't come home.' There was a brief pause. 'I'm your wife in name only.'

'You asked me to leave.'

'You should have known you needed to stay!' she shot back, and hissed out a breath.

His eyes widened at the show of temper and his heart quickened at the sight of her cheeks flushed with anger. She still took his breath away, he thought vaguely, and then his mind focused on her words.

'Is that what you really wanted?' he asked softly.

She pursed her lips. 'I don't want to talk about this, Jordan. What's done is done.'

'Clearly it isn't done. Tell me,' he begged. It had suddenly become imperative for him to know what he had walked away from. And whether she had wanted him to walk away at all.

'You made a choice to leave, Jordan.'

She looked up at him, her eyes piercing him with their fire. It wasn't a description he would have used of her before. And perhaps before he wouldn't have found it quite as alluring. But it suited her, he thought.

'We all have to live with the decisions we made then. For now, we need to focus on getting this event done.'

His jaw clenched and tension flowed through his body with his blood. She made it seem as though he had left easily—as though he had *wanted* to leave.

'I left because you asked me to. Why are you punishing me for it?'

She watched him steadily, and for a brief moment, he thought he saw her soften. But it was gone before he was sure, and then she answered him in a low voice.

'You're fooling yourself if you think you left because I asked you to.' She stopped, as though considering her words, and then continued, 'You left because you couldn't handle my grief.'

He felt his blood drain. 'Did my father tell you that?'

Mila frowned. 'Why would you think that?'

Because that was exactly what his father had accused him of in one of their last conversations before he'd left, Jordan thought in shock. After

Jordan had told Greg he was leaving—that Mila had asked him to and that he was going to Johannesburg to focus on getting their research institute started—his father had accused him of leaving because Mila's suffering had reminded Jordan of his mother's suffering. And that that meant Jordan was in the same position that his father had been in.

He had ignored the words when his father had said them—had believed the two situations had nothing in common—and had refused to think about it afterwards. But hearing those words come from Mila now brought the memory into sharp focus. But, just as he had then, Jordan shut down his thoughts and feelings about it.

'Do you think your contact would actually be able to make a customised marquee?'

He saw her blink, saw her adjust to his abrupt change in topic. She opened her mouth and closed it again, and then answered.

'Yes, I think he would.'

Her voice was polite. No, he thought, *controlled.*

'I think the more appropriate question would

be if he'd be able to do it in such a short period of time.'

She took her phone out and started typing, changing the tone of their conversation. The tension was still there though, he realised, noting the stiff movement of her fingers.

'If he *is* able to do it we'll have solved one of the major problems of this event.'

'I'm sure the others won't be quite as bad,' he said, and walked up the steps to the stage.

He needed space from her, even though she was standing a far enough distance away that her proximity shouldn't have bothered him. The stage was clear of the usual clutter events brought, he saw, with only the large white screen used for movies behind him.

'It's not going to be easy,' she warned. 'We'll have to see if the same food vendors are available, *and* we'll have to find out if Karen can perform...' She trailed off, as though the thought frightened her, and he felt the release of the tension in him at the memory of Mila dealing with the teenage singer.

'Won't *that* be fun for you?'

'I can't wait,' she said wryly. 'We might have

to consider someone else if she isn't available. After that, the hardest part is going to be getting people to come. Karen—or whoever we get to perform—will have a huge impact on that, but it's still going to be a challenge.'

'Social media will help,' he said, and walked down the stairs to where she stood. She was taking pictures, and he realised that with the marquee the space was different from what she'd worked with before. 'We can have Karen post something closer to the time. It could even be a pop-up concert.'

'That won't work,' she disagreed. 'Doing that would put us at risk of overcrowding or riots. Of course we can have her post about the event, but we need to sell tickets. That's the only way we can know how many people to expect.'

If he'd thought she wouldn't be insulted by it, he would have complimented her on her professional knowledge. But he'd learned his lesson the previous evening. He hadn't been around before to see her in action, but his father had complimented her often enough. Now Jordan could see why.

'Was it hard work the first time?'

She glanced over at him. 'Yes, but for different reasons. We had to start from scratch then. Design it, figure out what would work, what wouldn't. Now we don't have those problems, but we're working from a blueprint. Which means we're confined. It also puts us at risk of making a loss.'

'Well, regardless of that, we're going to have to plan this.' He stuck his hands into the pockets of his jacket. 'Maybe it's a good thing I wasn't here the first time.'

'Marketing wine in American restaurants does sound more exciting,' she said easily, and his heart knocked at hearing her attempt something remarkably close to banter. Perhaps they should stick to work, he thought.

'Well, seven of the ten restaurants I visited now carry our wines, so I *was* working. Besides, if I'd been here, we probably would have been married a lot earlier—' He broke off, cursing himself for not thinking. He almost saw Mila's walls go up again.

'This event is going to take a lot of work,' she said instead of addressing his slip. 'I might have to give Lulu a call...'

Her face had tightened, and Jordan wondered what he didn't know about Mila's only real friendship.

'Have you spoken to her recently?' he asked, watching the emotions play over her face.

'Now and then,' she answered him. 'Not nearly as often as I should have.'

The admission came as a surprise to him—and to her, too, it seemed.

'I think we've seen all we need to here.' she said quickly. 'The stairs…they're easier going up.'

It was a clear sign that she didn't want any help from him, and he had to clench his fists at his sides to keep himself from doing just that as he watched her painstakingly climb the stairs.

Why couldn't she just ask for help? he thought irritably, and then stilled when a voice asked him why she should need to ask at all.

CHAPTER FIVE

MILA HEARD THE door to the house slam and closed her eyes. Clearly Jordan hadn't returned from their trip to the amphitheatre in a good mood. Not that *she* was feeling particularly cheerful herself. She had let him bait her into lashing out, into revealing things she didn't want him to know.

It was only because she had been feeling particularly vulnerable after hesitating at those stairs. She had always hated that reminder of her accident—any reminder, really. But as she had stood in front of those steps, her heart in her throat, she had hated that the most. Because every time she thought she would be able to take a step she was reminded of the sensation of tumbling to the ground. Pain would flash through her at the memory of lying at the bottom of the steps, her breathing staggered, waiting for someone to help her.

She blamed that feeling for the accusation she had hurled at Jordan from nowhere earlier. She had never intended letting that slip—the *real* reason she thought he'd left—but her tongue no longer seemed to obey the 'think before you speak' rule she had always played by.

Heaven knew she was tired of taking all the blame for him leaving—yes, she *had* asked him for space, but that had been said in grief, in pain. She hadn't meant it, but when he'd packed his bags she hadn't been able to bring herself to ask him to stay. She had wanted him to—every fibre in her being had urged her to stop him—but she had also wanted him to *want* to stay. She had wanted him to refuse to go, to tell her that he needed her, to acknowledge that they needed *each other* to get through the heartbreak of losing their son.

But he hadn't, and she had been forced to admit to herself that their make-believe life—the one where they were playing at being a happy family and where she was a worthy wife—was never *really* going to be her life. Jordan hadn't had any reason to be with her before she had lost their baby, so why would he bother with her now, when she'd proved that she wasn't capable? When she'd proved that she was broken, especially during her grieving?

He must believe that, too, or he would never have asked her if Greg had told her that. Jordan must have said it to Greg at some point, in confidence, and the stunned expression she'd seen on his face must have been because Jordan had thought Greg had broken his confidence...

Hurt beat at her heart, but she set her shaking hands down on the lists of the things she needed to do and the notes from the phone calls she had made at the kitchen counter.

'Hey,' he said, and the deep voice made her heart jump in the same way it had when they'd first met.

She turned and saw the amicable expression on his face. Had she been mistaken about his mood? Perhaps not, she thought as she looked in his eyes.

'Hi,' she replied, determined not to let her emotions get in the way of amicability. If he could do it, so could she. 'You were gone for a while.'

'Yeah, I bumped into Frank and we talked about the vineyard. I got us some food, too.'

She could tell from his voice that something was bothering him, and while her heart wanted to ask him about it, her head told her to keep to the game they seemed to be playing.

'That was nice of you,' she said measuredly, and took the pizza from him.

It had already gone cold, she saw when she opened the boxes, making her wonder if he'd gone somewhere else after picking the food up. But she was distracted when she saw he had got her favourite pizza, and she had to force herself not to be swayed by something as simple as that that only indicated his memory.

'Frank couldn't have told you all that much,' she said, and took out two oven trays to warm the pizza on. 'You two spoke about the place quite often while you were gone.'

'Did he tell you that?'

She looked back at him, and was suddenly struck by how attractive he was. He'd taken off the red winter jacket he had on that morning, and now she was being treated to the sight of the muscles he sported almost lazily under his long-sleeved top. Even his light blue jeans highlighted the strength of his lower body.

She swallowed, and told herself to answer him instead of staring like a fool. 'Frank's mentioned it, yes. But he told your dad first, and Greg told me. I think he thought that if I knew you'd kept in touch, *I'd* get in touch with you.' She closed her eyes briefly as soon as she realised she'd said it. It was being in this kitchen with him, she thought, and desperately changed the topic. 'Do you want to eat now?'

'I'd like to take a shower first, but that shouldn't take too long.'

There was a pause, almost as if Jordan had wanted to say something else and then decided not to. She glanced at him and saw an unreadable expression on his face. That in itself told her something was bothering him, but still she refused to ask him. That wasn't supposed to be her job any more.

'This is different,' he said, abruptly changing the topic.

She followed his gaze and for the first time since Jordan had first brought her to his father's house she saw the brown cupboards and cream countertops. But since that was the part of the kitchen that *hadn't* changed, she knew he was referring to her new additions.

'I thought a little colour might cheer the place up.' She didn't add that she'd hoped it would cheer his father up, as well. Greg had always been a man of a few words, and often she'd thought that it was because of sadness. He hadn't ever spoken much about his wife—like father, like son—but when he had she'd seen that Greg had loved and missed her. And then in his ill health and missing Jordan, his sadness had become grumpiness and sometimes even meanness.

Jordan was watching her when she looked up, a complicated expression on his face, and she wondered if he realised what she hadn't said after all.

'I knew it would be something like that,' he said, and it sounded forced. 'I would never have pegged Dad as a fuchsia kind of guy.' He nodded his head to the curtains and matching utensils that were scattered across the counters.

She smiled a little, felt her guard ease a touch. 'I think he grew fond of it after a while. Though at the beginning he made all sorts of noises.' The smile widened. 'And then he started seeing how the colour lightened up the place, and how the art helped me, and he got much better then.'

The walls were covered with her mosaic artwork—something her doctor had once suggested she do to keep herself busy during a postaccident, postbaby check-up—and she was quite proud of it. It made her remember the simple things she had taken pleasure in before her life had been destroyed.

'How did it help you?'

He said the words so quietly that at first she didn't register what he'd asked. And then she realised that her guard was down, and her shoulders stiffened in response. *It shouldn't be this easy to slip up in front of him*, she thought. Not when slipping up meant talking to him about the time she was trying to move on from. Not when it meant him prodding her about it *again*.

'It just gave me something to keep busy with while I recovered,' she said firmly, and then turned to put the oven on and slide the trays with the pizzas into it.

She took her time with it, and it didn't take long for Jordan to get the picture. After a few moments, she heard the shower being turned on and she sighed with relief.

He was getting under her skin, she thought. He had always been able to do that to her, from the moment she had first taken that glass of wine from him two years ago. She'd forgotten all her insecurities then—had slipped into those enticing eyes of his and had believed that they would last, that she could be someone he wanted. Someone he needed.

The past didn't matter now, she thought, checking the pizzas. She had been young and completely in love then. Now she knew better. She could protect herself now—she *would* protect herself, regardless of how easy it seemed to be to slip up in front of him. Whether it was out of anger, or out of familiarity, she would control it.

A sharp pain snapped her from her thoughts, and she looked down to see an angry welt spread across her hand where she had reached for the oven tray without a mitt. She rolled her eyes as she ran the hand under cold water, blaming her silly thoughts for distracting her, but grateful that she had only used one hand instead of both, as she usually did.

Once the pain had subsided to a throb, she saw the welt was threatening to blister and rushed to the bathroom to get the first-aid kit and the gel she knew would soothe the burn.

She realised too late that Jordan was still in there, and barely had the chance to move back before the door opened. A cloud of steam followed a muscular body precariously covered by her white-and-pink towel out of the room.

'I'm so sorry! I was just—' She felt her face redden as she tried to avert her eyes from Jordan's half-naked body.

Except every time she tried, her eyes moved back to him of their own accord. She had been right when she'd thought his body was more muscular than she remembered. His broad shoulders were more defined, the muscles in his chest and abs sculpted so perfectly that she wondered if it were possible for her insides to burn, as well. Then she cleared her throat and told herself that she had seen him like this before. There was no reason to panic.

She took a deep breath. 'I'm sorry, I just need to get the first-aid kit.' She gestured to her hand and was quite proud of the way she'd managed to put words together in the calm tone her voice had taken.

Which all went out the window when he immediately walked to her and took her hand in his.

'What happened?'

'I...I burned myself.' Her mind was whirling at the feel of her hand in his, at the contact between them—however minimal. But her heart was the problem—it was thumping at a rhythm she thought she couldn't possibly sustain, merely because of his proximity.

'Still a clumsy cook, I see. Even when you're just heating pizza,' he said softly, and then he led her into the bathroom.

She had no choice but to stand there as he reached for the first-aid kit. He pulled out the soothing gel and spread it gently over her burn, and the heat went from her hand to the rest of her. His body was still warm from the shower, and she could smell his body wash—the same kind he'd used before they had broken up. The same kind that had thrilled her each time she had smelled it.

And suddenly her heart and her body longed

for him with an intensity that had her backing away from him.

'It's fine, thanks. I'll finish this up in the kitchen.' She grabbed the kit and almost ran back to the kitchen, not caring if he saw.

All she cared about was putting some distance between them so she could try and convince herself that he *wasn't* affecting her.

'Did you manage to call Lulu?' Jordan asked Mila when he'd finally got his body back under control.

He hadn't expected her to react like that after seeing him in a towel. The look she had given him before she had bolted had been filled with the desire that had marked their entire relationship, and his body had acted accordingly. But that was over now, he told himself, and he was making an effort to forget it. Except that all of a sudden he was noticing the curve of her neck, the faint blush of her cheeks...

'I did,' she replied, her voice husky, and he thought that maybe she wasn't as recovered as she pretended to be. 'She's coming over to the house tomorrow.'

Something in her voice made him forget about the curls that had escaped the clip she'd tied her hair back with. He looked up, saw the shaky hands that handed him his pizza and a glass of wine, and something pulled inside him.

'You're worried.'

'About seeing her?' She picked up her glass and plate, walking past him on her way to the lounge.

He followed, saw that she took one couch, and sat on the other. He didn't need another reason to be distracted by her. He watched as she broke a piece of pizza from the rest, but didn't lift it to her mouth.

'No, I think that's going to be fine,' she said, and lifted her head with a defiant smile.

But he could still see the uncertainty, and he knew that she was pretending. He just didn't know for whom.

'Do you really?'

'Yeah, of course. I mean, we've spoken in the last year.'

She was desperately trying to convince him— or perhaps again convince herself.

'Then why are you worried?' he asked again.

'And don't tell me you aren't because I can see that you are.'

'Honestly, it's nothing,' she replied, picking at her pizza, and he had to force himself not to be annoyed by her denials. He had to force himself not to push her just because he wanted to know. Because he wanted to help.

So he didn't answer her, biting from a slice of pizza that he didn't taste, chewing mechanically, waiting for her to speak. Her hands grew busier, and soon there was a pile of cheese on her plate and her pizza base was nearly bare. Still, he waited, because he could see it unnerved her, and perhaps it would do so enough that she would open up to him.

'I have to apologise.'

The words came out of nowhere, and Jordan felt a short moment of pride that his patience—a trait that maybe he needed more of—had paid off, before reacting to her words.

'Why?'

'I haven't...kept in touch with her like I should have. Not after the baby.'

She didn't look at him, and concern edged into his heart.

'You were in a difficult place.'

'And that's when you're supposed to *turn to* your friends, not push them away,' she said hotly, and then lifted a hand to her mouth as though she was surprised at her own words.

He could believe that, since it was the way he felt, too. Did she mean she shouldn't have pushed *him* away either?

'Maybe Lulu should have understood,' he replied carefully.

'Maybe,' she repeated. 'Maybe I expected her to.'

They were talking about the two of them, he knew, and yet he couldn't bring himself to speak plainly.

'You would have had to say it. How else would she have known?'

'Because she's my friend.'

You were my husband.

'She should have known.'

You should have stayed.

'People don't just know things, Mila,' he said with anger, the only emotion he was ready to accept. 'You have to tell them.'

'Because saying things means so much, right?' she replied calmly.

But he saw the ice in her eyes and he knew the calm was just a front.

'Like when you say things like "until death do us part"? That means you can never go back on it?' She raised her eyebrows, waiting for him to reply.

Just beneath his anger, he felt the guilt. When he had left he *had* gone back on his word. But he wouldn't have if she hadn't done it first.

'You said it, Mila. You have to turn to your friends when you need them, not push them away. *You* were the first one to go back on your word.'

Her eyes widened, and it seemed that for a moment the ice melted as a tear fell down her cheek. She wiped it away and stood.

'This was a mistake. Pretending we could do something as simple as having a meal together without getting into some kind of argument.' She slammed her plate onto the coffee table. 'Neither of us may be innocent in what happened between us, but don't for one moment think I went back on my word. *I* lost our baby. *My* body failed us. So when I asked for space I was racked with guilt. I was *devastated*. But you didn't even fight. You left like it was the easiest decision you ever made.'

'It was the *hardest* decision I ever made,' he shot back, setting his plate next to hers and standing, too, his body riddled with tension, with emotion. 'But it was better for me to focus on my work, on something I could control.' He frowned at the unexpected admission, and shook his head. 'It was the best decision, Mila.'

'For who, Jordan? You or me?'

She wiped at another tear and it pierced his heart.

'This is so silly. I'm going to bed. I'll see you in the morning.'

He couldn't bring himself to ask her to stay— knew that if he did he needed to say something other than the accusations that were coursing through his mind.

When he heard her bedroom door close he flopped down on the couch, thinking about her words. She'd wanted him to stay. The realisation was a blow to his heart that he didn't know he could recover from, and the niggling in the back of his mind—the niggle that had always made him doubt his decision to leave—finally gained ground.

He *had* believed that he was doing the right thing for her. But her words now made him wonder if it had been only for her, or for him, too. His own words seemed to prove that it had.

He thought about how relieved he had been to focus on something he could control, to focus on his work. Unlike the day when Mila had fallen and he'd had no choice but to sign the forms approving the emergency C-section. Unlike the subsequent loss of his son that he'd been unable to do anything about, just as he had been able to do nothing about Mila's grief and suffering.

He froze as his father's accusation about why he'd left played back in his head. For the first time he considered it. If Jordan *had* left Cape Town—had left the wife who'd needed him—because it reminded him of his mother's illness, then Jordan *had* been running. When Mila had asked him for space to deal with the tragedy of losing their child he had run away. From her pain...from his. Because he hadn't wanted to see her suffer—emotionally or physically—as his mother had. Because he didn't want to watch on, helpless, as his father had.

Pain stabbed through him and he rested his head in his hands. Were those the *real* reasons he had left?

CHAPTER SIX

MILA WOULD HAVE liked a day to ignore the world and lick her wounds. To ignore the fact that the tension between her and Jordan was making her feel ill. She knew that she was causing it—that if she could just sit back and agree as she had during their marriage, she wouldn't be in the situation she was.

But words kept pouring from her mouth as if she had no control over them. Maybe because she'd realised control didn't *do* anything. Jordan had still left, even though she had done—and said—everything she'd *supposed* to. She had managed to alienate her best friend—her *only* friend—even though she had always gone out of her way to make sure everyone liked her. To make sure she would always have someone who wanted her.

But when the doorbell rang the next morning she knew that she wouldn't be able to wallow. Not only because she had to meet Lulu, but because the meeting was only a part of what she needed to do for the event.

She'd made some progress—Karen's manager had told her that he would run the event by the singer and confirm after that. Her marquee contact had agreed to the customised design, his complaints about the short timeline quelled by the generous amount of money she'd offered. And on her to-do list that day was getting in touch with the food vendors and checking their availability for the next month. That and Karen would determine the date of the event, and once that was confirmed she would be able to start the marketing process.

Before she could get to that list, though, she needed to face Lulu.

Her hands were shaking as she made her way to the front door. She took a deep breath before she opened it, and then she smiled.

'Hi!' she said, and her eyes swept over Lulu.

Her first thought was that Lulu hadn't changed all that much. Her face was still oval shaped, her hair cut close to her head. Her brown skin was smooth, her light brown eyes careful as she looked at Mila. Her second thought was that none of that mattered when there was something massive that *had* changed.

'You're pregnant...' Mila said through frozen lips, and her heart sped up. Her breath threatened to speed up, too, but she saw the reserve in Lulu's eyes change to concern and forced herself to control it.

It was just one of those annoying reactions she'd had since losing her baby—like the stairs. She was strong enough to deal with the reaction her body had to seeing Lulu pregnant. Strong enough for the emotional one, too. So she ignored the heartache, the emptiness, and clung to the genuine excitement she felt for her friend.

'Congratulations!'

She pulled Lulu into a hug, ignoring the distance that had grown between them since her fall. She also ignored the way the swell of Lulu's belly made her feel incredibly empty.

'How far along are you?'

Lulu squeezed Mila quickly and then pulled back. The concern still gleaming in Lulu's eyes was almost eclipsed by the reserve that had now returned. 'Thank you. I'm twenty-eight weeks. I wasn't sure if I should come because of…'

Her voice grew softer as she spoke, and Mila knew exactly what Lulu was saying.

'Well, I'm glad you came. Please come inside.'

Lulu walked past her and Mila closed her eyes for a second. Lulu had kept her pregnancy from Mila for more than six months because she had been afraid of the way Mila would react. What did that say about her? she thought, and her heart felt bruised at the knowledge. She had never meant for her tragedy to keep her friend from telling her the happy news. It meant Mila had more to atone for than she'd originally thought.

'Is there anything I can get you? Some tea or coffee?'

'Um…no, thank you. I can't stay too long,' Lulu said, and Mila realised that she wouldn't have time to beat around the bush.

She watched Lulu gingerly lower herself onto one of the couches, and briefly thought that she remembered that perfectly. But she shook her head and decided she wasn't going to go down that path.

Instead, she spoke. 'Look, I know things be-

tween us aren't like they used to be. Our work
has suffered because of…everything that happened to me…and now that I know you're pregnant I feel even worse about not taking on more
so we could get commission—'

'I'm not interested in our work, Mila,' Lulu interrupted, her pretty face tense. 'Our *friendship*
has suffered.'

Hearing Lulu say that made Mila feel worse.
'I know. I…I should have called.'

'You should have,' Lulu agreed. 'And you
shouldn't have pushed me away at all. We've been
friends for almost a decade.'

'I know,' Mila said again, and felt herself dan-
gerously close to tears. It was almost the same
conversation she had had with Jordan the previous night. And it was time she admitted the truth
of it to herself.

'I just…' She stopped. Took a breath. Tried
again. 'I couldn't deal with it. I didn't want people
around me who would remind me of the things
I'd failed at.'

Lulu didn't respond, and Mila didn't look
up to see what her friend's face might tell her.

She didn't deserve the benefit of the doubt, she thought harshly.

'How would Jordan and I have done that?' Lulu asked finally, with a slight hitch to her voice that told Mila she was hurt. Her heart panged.

'I wasn't a good enough wife or a good enough mother, Lulu. Can't you see that?' Mila was suddenly desperate to make her understand. 'I should have taken it easy, like Jordan asked me to...' She faltered, but then continued, 'I didn't want Jordan around to remind me of how I had failed.'

'Even if that made sense—which it absolutely does not—why did you push *me* away? I wanted to be there for you.'

A trickle of heat ran down Mila's face. 'I know you did. But I didn't deserve someone around who wanted me to feel better about myself.'

'Oh, Mila...'

Lulu walked to where she was standing and pulled Mila into her arms. On autopilot, Mila returned the hug, too busy thinking about what she had just revealed to her friend—to herself— to be really present in the moment.

'You deserve everything. Happiness...love.' Lulu pulled back, her eyes teary. 'You *are* good enough. You just need to give yourself permission to believe that.'

Though she wanted to, Mila didn't waste her breath on asking how she could do that.

'I'm a mess,' Lulu said suddenly, wiping at her eyes. 'Pregnancy hormones are *very* real.'

'Yes, they are,' Mila replied, smiling, but then the smile faded. 'I'm sorry about everything, Lulu. I shouldn't have... Well, I should have let you be my friend.'

'Yeah, you should have.' Lulu watched her for a moment. 'Friends are *there* for one another, Mila. I don't know how after almost ten years you still don't know I'm not going anywhere.'

Because for almost double that time I didn't have anyone to show me what that meant.

But she simply repeated, 'I'm sorry.'

'Apology accepted,' Lulu said, and then sat down again. 'So—tell me the other reason you called.'

A genuine smile crept across her lips. 'How did you know?'

Lulu gave her a look that had Mila's smile spreading.

'I want to start working again. Seriously, this

time. Again, I'm sorry I let the ball drop with all the events we should have been doing—'

'Oh, I've been doing them anyway,' Lulu interrupted.

'You have?'

Lulu shrugged. 'It didn't seem right to let things fall apart just because you needed some time to recover. So I've been responding to emails from the website and I forwarded you some so that you'd have something to do.'

Another smile crept onto Mila's face. 'You've been *managing* me?'

Lulu let out a small laugh. 'Yes, maybe I have. But it's meant that your business hasn't fallen apart.'

'Like my personal life, you mean?' The smile on Mila's face faltered before she reminded herself that she needed to move on. 'Thank you, Lulu. That means more than you know.'

'It wasn't a big deal. All the details, including the financials are in this binder.' Lulu reached into her bag—puffing just a little, since it was on the floor—and handed Mila the file. She took it, but didn't look inside. She trusted Lulu, and knew everything would be in order.

'I already have our next event,' Mila said, and explained about the event they needed to plan, the timeline and what she'd already done.

She absorbed Lulu's shock at the details, and was immensely grateful when Lulu didn't comment on the fact that she was doing the event with Jordan...or the fact that they were still married. At least that was what she thought.

But after they had spoken about the event in more detail, and just as Lulu was on her way out, her friend said, 'You know, I was with you when you met Jordan *and* when you found out you were pregnant. I saw how happy both of those things made you. How happy being a family made you. Maybe finding out you're still married is a sign for you to try again. A second chance.'

Mila ignored the hope, the fierce desire that sprang up inside her at Lulu's words. 'That's not going to happen.'

'Why not? You still love him. I know you do. And you've always wanted a family, so...' Lulu trailed off.

'That doesn't matter any more, Lulu,' Mila said firmly. 'I just want to move on with my life.

Focus on my work. Be a good aunt.' She tried to smile.

Lulu shook her head. 'If that's what you really want, I'll support you. But just make sure it *is* what you really want. And do me a favour?'

Mila looked up at her.

'Give yourself permission to think about what you want *honestly.*'

'Yeah, I will,' Mila responded, and then took the time to enjoy having a moment with the only person who had made her feel loved since she was sixteen.

No, that's not true, she thought, and heard Lulu's words about Jordan, about family, echo in her head.

Was a second chance possible?

No. She clamped down on the thought. She couldn't go down that path. Not if she wanted to survive the task they'd been given.

CHAPTER SEVEN

JORDAN WAS RETURNING from his morning run just as Lulu came out through the front door.

'Hey!' she exclaimed when she saw him, and Jordan grinned, remembering how much fun she had always been.

She and Mila had been a bundle of light together. It bothered him to see how much of that light had dimmed in Mila, he thought as he saw her, too, and his smile faded.

'You look great, Lulu,' he said, focusing his attention on the pretty woman in front of him. And then he saw that she was pregnant and his heart clenched. He suddenly became aware of the way his lungs struggled for air, the way his shoulders felt heavy with grief. He cleared his throat. 'Congratulations.'

'Thanks,' she said softly, and he saw the flash of concern in her eyes.

Because he didn't need it, he forced out,

'You finally managed to find someone who deserves you?'

'Yeah—still my husband.'

She smiled at him kindly and then turned back to Mila, who was watching their exchange with wary eyes.

'Let me know how this afternoon goes. Like I said, most of the vendors will be there. And I'll track down those who aren't.'

'Thanks.' Mila's eyes warmed as she looked at Lulu. 'I'll see you soon.'

They both stood and watched as Lulu walked to her car, and waved at the sound of her horn. When she was no longer in sight Jordan felt his legs go weak, and he walked forward to the chair that stood next to the front door.

'Hey...' Mila crouched down in front of him, and as his heart palpitated and he fought for a steady breath, she took his hand and squeezed. 'Look at me. *Look* at me, Jordan,' she repeated when he didn't respond the first time.

He lifted his eyes.

'You're going to be okay. Just keep breathing.'

She repeated it until finally he could feel his heart falling back into the uncomfortable rhythm it always had around her. He pulled his hand away, embarrassed at his reaction. She stood up, but his hope that she would leave it alone and go inside faltered when she took the seat next to him.

'So it happens to you, too?'

He looked over at her, but she was staring out to where the trees lined the driveway.

'I don't know what you're talking about.'

'Your lungs feel like they don't work any more and your heart feels like it's beating to keep the entire world alive.'

She still wasn't looking at him and he eased. He didn't know why he had reacted to Lulu in that way. He had seen other pregnant women before. Why had this one been any different?

'It's happened to you?' he said hoarsely before he could stop himself.

'Yeah, plenty of times.' She paused. 'It almost happened with Lulu today.'

'Why didn't it?'

'I didn't want her to think I wasn't happy for her.'

He nodded. He understood that. And perhaps for the first time he found himself opening up the door he had locked his feelings about his son's death behind.

'I don't know why this is different.'

'Because she's someone you know. You care about her,' she answered softly. 'It hits harder when it's closer to home.'

'Yeah, probably,' he agreed, but something told him there was something else, as well.

'I know what I said, but it doesn't mean that you're not happy for her.'

He knew she was looking at him, so he nodded, but didn't respond. Pieces were settling in his mind from where he had locked them away. And then he spoke almost without realising it.

'You're right. When I saw Lulu there was a part of me that was happy for her before the doom and gloom set in.' He realised now where the reaction had come from, and for some reason felt comfortable with saying it out loud. He didn't care to examine why.

'And...?' Mila prompted softly.

'And I felt bad about it because when we found out *you* were pregnant...' he couldn't quite believe he was saying it '...I was terrified.'

'What?' The shocked tone of her voice had his heart accelerating.

'Of course, I was happy, too. But I was scared.'

'You never told me that.'

'You were so happy. I didn't want to spoil that.'

'I was scared, too, Jordan.' She let out a little laugh when he looked at her. 'I didn't know the first thing about being a mother. About being in a family.'

His mouth opened in surprise, but before she could see it, he asked, 'Why didn't you tell me?'

'Because *you* were so happy.' She smiled over at him. 'I didn't want you to think I couldn't do it.'

Something bothered him about her answer. It reminded him of the time she'd thought he was telling her she wasn't good at her job.

'I never thought that,' he said. 'I knew you were going to be a wonderful mother.'

'You would have been a wonderful father, too.'

'Maybe,' he replied.

Or maybe he would have been as emotionally unavailable as his own father had been. He frowned, but didn't ponder it any more. Not when he was thinking about how nice it was sitting with her. The grief he'd felt at seeing the chairs where he'd spent so much time with his father for the first time after Greg's death had faded, and he knew it was because of Mila. She was the only person besides his father that he wanted to be there with.

The realisation unsettled him.

'Why were you scared?' She interrupted his thoughts. 'I mean, I know becoming a parent is scary in general, but was that the only thing?'

No, he thought, but he couldn't bring himself to say it when he was only just beginning to re-alise the effect his parents had had on him. Like the fact that part of his fear over becoming a par-ent was because of the way his father had treated him as a child—fear that he would turn out just like that.

'Yeah, that's all.'

He looked over at her and saw that she didn't believe him. Saw the flash of hurt in her eyes be-cause of it, felt the nudge in his heart. And still he couldn't formulate the words.

'It didn't seem like things went poorly with Lulu,' he said instead, hoping for reprieve.

'They didn't,' she replied in a measured tone,

and he closed his eyes when he realised he might just have undone the progress they'd made. In their *working* relationship, he clarified to himself.

'So, you guys are friends again?'

'We were never *not* friends, it seems. She's even been doing events for me while I've been...away.'

'That's great,' he said lamely, and felt helpless as the tension seeped back in between them. Silence came with it, giving him enough time to berate himself for spoiling the tentative truce that they'd been starting to forge.

But he couldn't tell Mila why he hadn't told her everything. She didn't know that side of his father, and he didn't want to taint her memories of Greg by telling her about the angry person his father had been in Jordan's youth. About the remnants of that time that had marred his relationship with his father right up to Greg's death. And now Jordan would never get the chance to fix it, or to make up for the past year when he hadn't been in touch...

'Lulu told me about a food fair that's happening this afternoon.' She broke the silence. 'It's at the Johnson High School in town—and most of the vendors who were there for the original Under the Stars are going to be there. I'm leaving in an hour. You can come, if you like.'

'I'd like that very much. I'll go get ready,' he said softly, grateful that she was still trying to be amicable despite his reluctance to open up to her.

As he headed to the bathroom for a shower he thought about it. He hadn't told her much about his childhood. Their relationship had been such a whirlwind at the beginning, and he'd fallen in love with her before he'd known what was happening. And then they'd got married, just three months after meeting—Jordan couldn't remember *ever* making such an impulsive decision—and Mila had fallen pregnant a few months after that.

Things had been so anchored in the future for them that they hadn't considered their past. They hadn't considered how the way they had grown up and how the people in their lives might have an impact on their relationship.

It made him realise that there were pieces between them that had been broken long before they'd lost their child. They hadn't even been able to share the way they'd felt about having a baby, for crying out loud! Each of them hadn't wanted to offend the other with their real feelings. That wasn't a healthy relationship.

The conversation they had just had was the first open one they'd had since they'd met—at least about their pasts. Did that mean things were changing for them? Did he *want* them to? He couldn't deny how being with Mila reminded him of how much he had felt for her. Maybe *still* felt for her...

No! He shut that train of thought down as the water hit his body. There was no point in exploring that now. His marriage was over in every way but legally. He would just focus on the event, on helping Mila, and then on running the vineyard in a way that would have made his parents proud.

He *would* focus on that, Jordan told himself when the hope inside him twinged.

There was no point in hoping after all that had happened between them.

CHAPTER EIGHT

SHE NEEDED TO THINK.

She couldn't turn to the usual activities that helped her to do so since they all involved staying in the house with Jordan, so Mila decided to go to the place that always did.

She grabbed her jacket and walked out into the sunshine that was growing rarer the closer it got to winter. Though the cold air reminded her of the season, it brought a beauty to the vineyard that was underappreciated. *Especially from here*, she thought, standing atop the slope that overlooked the vineyard, just as she had the previous day with Jordan.

It felt as if it were a lot longer than that. So much had happened since then. She'd done a lot for the event, yes, but she had also learned a lot about herself. About how much she wanted to look worthy, and how she had sacrificed her relationships in pursuit of that. About how much

what people thought about her affected her be-
haviour—and how she couldn't bring herself to
acknowledge that to herself, or to the people who
cared about her.

Perhaps it was because there hadn't been many
people who cared about her when she was growing up. She'd had ten different foster families
over her years of being in foster care, and she
couldn't remember even one of them fostering
because they actually *cared* about the children
they were looking after.

It meant that she desperately wanted to feel
loved, to feel needed. But it also meant that she
didn't know how to turn to people when she
needed *them*. Her conversation with Lulu had
shown her that those were opposing desires, since
the people she wanted to feel loved and needed
by needed to feel that, too. And, since she struggled to do that, she only succeeded in pushing
them away. It was a vicious cycle, and if she was
being honest with herself, it was another reason
the loss of her baby had broken her.

When she'd fallen pregnant so quickly, so un-
expectedly, she had let herself hope for a family. She was going to have a child—someone

who would need her without conditions. Someone who would know that she needed them, too, without her having to say it. That was what family was, wasn't it?

But she had also been scared that she wouldn't be a good mother. And of the way having a baby would change her life. In some ways it had been a remnant of her fears about marriage. Her pregnancy seemed to have sharpened them, causing her to worry that they'd moved too fast.

So she had clung to her job, working just as hard as she had before she'd fallen pregnant to prove to herself that things wouldn't change that much. She'd ignored Jordan's suggestion that she move more slowly, that she take time to adjust to the changes her body and their lives were going through.

And then she'd fallen down the stairs and her baby had been born prematurely, only surviving for seventeen minutes in the world Mila was supposed to have prepared him for. Her mourning had been part grief at her loss, part guilt at the fact that she hadn't slowed down. That she'd put her selfish fears first.

And in her grief she'd realised how unimportant

those fears had been. Having a family—having her son—had always been the most important. She'd pushed Jordan, Greg and Lulu away because that realisation had come too late, and she hadn't wanted to be reminded of how stupid she'd been.

So she'd locked her hopes for a family away, convincing herself that she could survive without one. And she would cling to that belief so no one would get hurt again because of her. It didn't matter what Lulu said about second chances and Mila wanting more. Wanting more didn't matter. Not any more.

Besides, she and Jordan just weren't right for each other. She absently rubbed at the ache that throbbed in her chest at the thought as she remembered their interaction earlier. She'd had no idea he was as affected as she was by their baby's death, and she felt awful about it. She could still see the way the colour had leached from his face when he'd realised Lulu was pregnant, could still remember how erratic his breathing had been.

It always gave her an objective glimpse into what other people felt when she went through her own episodes, and it wasn't good. And, though she still felt guilt about it, knowing that he struggled, too, made her feel a little better about how she was coping. It made her feel, for the first time since her life had imploded in front of her, as if she wasn't alone.

But that didn't mean anything other than shared experience, she thought firmly. She and Jordan hadn't even shared the way they'd really felt about having a baby. And then she had told him about why *she* hadn't, about why *she* was scared, and he had still refused to share *his* feelings with her. It reminded her of how little she actually knew about him...

No, she concluded. They weren't right for each other. And no matter what her heart said she couldn't be with someone who didn't want to let her in.

'Going down?' a voice asked behind her, and she turned, her heart in her throat until she realised that it was Frank, not Jordan behind her.

'No.' She smiled at him and checked her watch. 'I have under thirty minutes before I need to leave to do some work on the event. There's no time for me to get lost in the fields today.'

Frank nodded and just stood behind her, and his steady presence gave her a feeling of calm.

'Something's wrong,' Frank said, still staring out to the fields.

She bit her lip when Frank's lack of eye contact reminded her of how uncomfortable he was talking about anything personal, and answered him. 'Nothing out of the ordinary.'

Not if you counted a will forcing you to reunite with a not-so-ex-husband as ordinary.

'You sure?'

'Yes.' She turned to him now, and saw the concern on his face. 'I'm not going to break down because Jordan is back, Frank.'

Frank sank his hands into his pockets and shifted his weight. He hated interfering, she thought, and her heart warmed even as she wondered why he thought he needed to.

'I know you're a strong, independent woman...'

This time Mila didn't try to hide her smile.

'But that doesn't mean that your ex being back shouldn't bother you in some way.'

Her smile faded and she shrugged. 'I'm not saying it doesn't bother me. But I can handle it.'

'He hurt you pretty bad the last time.'

'Yeah, he did. But I hurt him, too,' she answered without thinking, and lifted a hand to her mouth when she realised it was true. She *had* hurt him when she'd asked him to give her space. The thought left a feeling of discomfort in her stomach.

'I can talk to him if you like.'

She smiled. 'You would hate that.'

Frank returned her smile. 'I would. But I'd do it.'

'I know you would. For Greg, right?' She said it because she knew it must be true. Especially since Greg had asked her to look after the others at the vineyard in the same way.

'Yeah. But for you, too.'

She brushed a kiss on Frank's cheek because she knew he cared for her, and laughed when the action made him blush.

'I'm okay, Frank. I promise.'

She left after that, the brief interaction leaving her steadier. Perhaps it was because she believed what she'd told Frank. She *could* handle Jordan.

Yes, his being back brought back emotions, memories that she wished she could forget. And it stirred up the anger, the accusations she'd wanted to hurl at him the moment she'd got the divorce papers that had made her realise he had given up on them. But the more time she spent with him now also made her realise that there were things between them that had never really been right. With her, with him or in their relationship.

But Frank's presence had reminded her of the promise she'd made to Greg to look after the vineyard. And for the first time she realised the implications of Greg's will on that promise. If she didn't put aside her feelings, she wouldn't be able to plan the event. That would mean that 50 per cent of the vineyard would be auctioned off, which would mean an uncertain future.

If someone horrible became part-owner, it would affect Frank and everyone else on the vineyard that she'd grown to care about. She *had* to do it for them. She needed to plan this event, make sure that it was a success and then sign her share over to Jordan even if the whole process pained her.

And she would do it for the people she cared about.

It seemed to Jordan that he wasn't the only one who had decided to let his feelings take a back seat. Mila had greeted him cordially when she'd seen him waiting for her on one of the chairs on the patio and asked him to drive them to the school. Her tone had been reserved, but not entirely cold, and Jordan had thought that maybe she had decided cordiality was better than letting the emotions of the past interfere again.

He couldn't agree more, and so an unspoken truce had formed between them. He'd waited for Mila to grab some things from her room, and when she'd returned and walked past him the smell of vanilla had followed her. His body had tightened in response, and he'd wondered how difficult this truce would be.

'What's our plan for this?'

'Well, I have the list of all the vendors we used last time. Most of them will be at this food fair— thank goodness Stellenbosch's event industry is small—so we can split up and ask them about their availability and interest in our event.'

He ran his tongue over his teeth, keeping his eyes glued to the road. 'I don't think we should split up. Didn't the will stipulate we do this together?'

She gave him a wry smile. 'I don't think that's what your father meant.'

'Maybe not, but it would probably be a good idea for me to tag along with you. I didn't do any of this the first time, remember?'

He wasn't sure when it had suddenly become so important for him to stay with her—especially since he was sure he could convince a few vendors to come to an event that they would get great publicity and payment for.

'Fine, we can stay together.'

She said it as though she was conceding millions instead of just her company. Was there a reason she didn't want to spend time with him? Maybe it was because she could also feel the slight sizzle that simmered between them whenever they were together.

'It would probably be best if I introduce you as the new owner of the vineyard. It might give some of them more incentive to say yes.'

'And what happens after this?'

'We speak to Karen—she's supposed to contact me to confirm if she can do it.'

He glanced over at her, saw the pained expression on her face, and smiled. 'Brings back bad memories, does it?'

She groaned, and it made him feel lighter than he had in a while. 'I've always thought about her with both pride and despair. Her performance that night was fantastic, but I could have done without the drama.'

'But if she *can* perform…?'

'We'll have to work with her to figure out a date. And then we market.'

They had just pulled up at the school, and were being directed up a road that Jordan remembered led to a sports field. It was ages since he'd been here, he thought idly, and then turned his attention back to Mila when she spoke.

'Did you know she's playing a concert? Saturday at Westgate Stadium. It would be an excellent way to show our support. You up for it?'

His eyebrows rose. 'You want me to go with you?'

'If I have to suffer through a concert with a load of teenagers, then so do you, buddy.'

He grinned, and found himself relaxing for the first time since he'd arrived back home. 'Sounds fair to me.'

They got out after he'd parked, and he took a moment to appreciate the beauty of the surroundings he'd in no way appreciated in his teens. The field he stood on reminded him of the countless rugby matches he'd played there, and though nostalgia was easy to slip into, he found the scene beyond the school to be more compelling.

The hills made it seem almost enclosed by nature, and had been the backdrop to many of his teenage escapades. Large trees were scattered over the grounds, leaves fading from green to orange with the turn of the season. He thought it might only be in Cape Town that even a school was beautiful to look at.

'This place hasn't changed since I was here,' Jordan said as they stood in line to get tickets, and he watched as Mila turned her head to follow his gaze.

'The swimming pool is new,' Mila pointed out, and he looked over and saw she was right.

He wasn't sure how he had missed that, since the school grounds were built at a much lower level than where they were parked.

'How do you know the pool's new?'

'I went to school here, too,' she said, a light blush covering her cheeks.

He wondered why telling him that would embarrass her. He frowned. 'Why didn't we see each other?'

'You would have been four years ahead of me, so we would have only seen each other if I was there in your last year.' She glanced over at him. 'I wasn't.'

'So you came after I had already matriculated.' The timeline had already formed in his head.

'Yeah, and only stayed for a year.'

'And then what?'

'I got moved to another family and another school.'

Her words left him...disconcerted. Perhaps it was because of the reminder of her childhood. Or perhaps it was because she had never spoken about her schooling before. It highlighted another crack in the relationship they'd had before breaking up. Shouldn't he have known this about her, his wife?

'Why didn't I know this?'

She shrugged, though the gesture was made

with stiff shoulders, and the relaxation Jordan had felt only a few moments ago slipped away.

'There were a lot of things we didn't talk about, Jordan,' she said.

Exactly what he'd realised over the past few days, he thought. He took out his wallet before Mila could pay when they got to the front of the line, and turned to her as they waited for their tickets.

'It seems a bit strange that we didn't talk about it, doesn't it…?'

He trailed off when he saw that her face had lost its colour. And then he realised why. Because the school was at a lower level, there was a long staircase that led down to another sports field. It was steep, even for him, and he felt her shake even before he saw it.

'I can't do this,' she said, and turned away, her eyes wide and frightened.

Jordan felt the punch to his stomach even as steel lined it. 'You don't have a choice,' he said firmly, and grabbed her hand, leading her to the stairs slowly.

Every step she took—every uncertain, painful step—sliced at his heart, but he knew he had to do this for her. He knew that if he could redeem himself in any way for the decisions he'd made since the day she'd fallen down the stairs, it would be by giving her back her freedom. And he knew her well enough to know that the only way to do that was through tough love.

'Jordan, please...' she whispered, her hand white on the railing. She had managed one step down the stairs, but had then frozen.

'Mila, look at me.' He waited as she did so, letting those behind him pass as he stood with Mila. 'You *have* to do this. The event depends on it. The vineyard depends on it. For my father.'

It was a low blow and he knew it, and he saw the responding flash of red in her eyes. But the look quickly fizzled out as he took her hand again, and was replaced by a combination of fear and...trust? he thought, and felt that punch in his gut again.

He couldn't ponder why that look had that effect on him now, though, and instead focused on taking another step down, waiting for her to join him. After taking a breath, she did. He saw the temptation in her eyes to freeze again, and decided that distracting her would soften the tough-love approach.

'Do you think it's because we did everything so fast that we didn't talk about our pasts?' he asked her, and patted himself on the back when he saw confusion in her eyes at his change of topic.

'That was a part of it.' Her voice was shaky, but she had taken the next step with his encouragement. 'But definitely not the biggest part.'

'What do you mean?'

She rolled her eyes, and he thought vaguely that his attempt at distraction was working. Except that she was distracting *him*, too.

'We told each other about the most important parts. You knew that I didn't have any family, and that I grew up in foster care, and I knew that your mom had passed away from cancer.'

'And we were just content with that...' he said, more to himself than to her.

Ever since he had realised that there had been things in their relationship that were broken even before the accident, the more he saw them. Yes, they'd known the basics—like the fact that her father had died before she was born and her mother had died shortly after her birth—but he'd had no idea how that had made her *feel*. Just as she hadn't known how his mother's death had affected him. And how much he blamed himself for it.

'*You* were,' she scoffed, and took another step down, still leaning on him. 'I wanted to know everything about you. About your father, your mother, your childhood... *Everything*,' she repeated. 'But you didn't seem willing to offer the information...'

She took a deep breath, but he knew it had little to do with the fact that she was going down the stairs.

'And I never wanted to push.'

He frowned. 'You didn't *want* to ask me about my life?'

She was silent for a moment. 'I didn't want to push you to give me any information you didn't want to.'

'Why not?'

She looked at him, uncertainty flickering in her eyes. 'Because I didn't want to tell *you* things either.'

It was a strange conversation to be having while she was facing her fears, he thought briefly, but in that moment the only thing that had his attention was what she was saying.

'What didn't you want to tell me?'

He felt her hand tighten, felt her resistance as she tried to pull away from him, but then she stopped. Maybe because she'd realised that pulling away from him would mean she would have to deal with her fear alone. Or maybe because she had chosen to be cordial and her refusal to answer his question would be going against that. But still she didn't say anything.

'Why did it embarrass you to tell me that you went to school here?' he asked, with a sudden urgency lighting up inside him that made it imperative for him to know. The same urgency that told him that whatever she didn't want to tell him about her life was somehow tied to that.

'It didn't,' she replied quickly. Too quickly for someone who had only a few minutes ago stiffened next to him.

'Mila...' It was a plea—one that came from that urgency—and it seemed to make a dent in that defensiveness she'd always had about her past. One he was beginning to realise *he* had, too.

She let out a huff. 'I just didn't want you to

think about my crappy unstable childhood when you'd had the complete opposite.'

'That embarrassed you?' he asked incredulously, and a wave of shame washed through him. Had he said something to her that had made her feel embarrassed about her childhood? Did she really think his had been so wonderful?

'Yes, it did,' she said through gritted teeth. 'You had an amazing home—one you could go to every day. You had a father who loved you. I had none of that.'

'Why were you embarrassed by that?'

'Because...' She had reached the bottom of the stairs, but she didn't seem to notice. She took another breath, and said, 'Because it meant that I wasn't worthy of someone like you.'

CHAPTER NINE

THE WORDS HAD already left Mila's lips when she realised how much they revealed about her. She was annoyed that it was the second time she had disclosed something to Jordan that she hadn't wanted him to know, even if it had made her feel better. Especially since the disturbed look on his face made her think that he didn't feel like what she'd said.

'Did you really believe that?' he asked softly.

'I did.'

Maybe I still do.

'It doesn't matter any more, though, does it?'

'You're wrong, you know.' He shook his head. 'I haven't met anyone else I respect more than you. You didn't have family, but you're more loyal than any family member I can think of. Even me.'

He paused, and she thought that he was sacrificing his own comfort to make her feel better. It melted her heart.

'You looked after my father when I couldn't. Thank you.'

His words made her blush, and she mumbled, 'You know you don't have to thank me for that.'

'I know you don't think I need to—which just proves my point. You *are* worthy, Mila. *I'm* the one who isn't worthy of *you*.' He shook his head. 'I didn't have the childhood you thought I did.'

'What do you mean?'

He stuffed his hands into his pockets and looked down. The gesture made him look so defeated she wanted to hold him in her arms, but as she followed his gaze she realised she was looking at grass. She'd made it down the stairs!

'I did it…' she said to herself, not quite believing this victory, especially after the fear had paralysed her for over a year.

'Yeah, you did.'

Jordan smiled at her, and for the first time since he had returned, she could tell that it was completely genuine, despite the look of disconcertion on his face.

'I did it. I really did it.'

She felt like a fool when her eyes started tearing up, but she couldn't help it. A small piece inside her that had broken after she'd lost her son had become whole, and it gave her a sense of peace. She felt relief, a sense of accomplishment, and so many other emotions she couldn't even begin to put her finger on.

When she looked at Jordan, she saw that his frown had cleared, replaced by a look of satisfaction.

He did this purposely, she thought and, ignoring the voice that screamed in her head, she hugged him.

The comfort of it hit her so hard that she had to close her eyes. But that only heightened her senses. The woodsy smell of him was intoxicating—so familiar and masculine that awareness heated inside her. She was moulded to his body, could feel the strength of the muscles she had admired when she'd first seen him after he'd returned. His arms—which had been still at his sides until that moment—wrapped around her and she was pulled in tighter to his body. Her breathing slowed, her heart sped up, and she had to resist the urge to pull his head down so that she could taste his lips.

And then she lifted her head and met his eyes. The heat of longing there was a reflection of her own, and she could feel the world fade as it always did with him. Gooseflesh shot out on her skin, and she considered for a brief moment what would happen if she kissed him.

It would be magical, she knew. The things inside her that had died when he'd left would find life. She would finally feel alive again. *But at what cost?* a voice asked her, and she took a step back from him, knowing that it would take away everything she had rebuilt if she gave in to this temptation.

'Thank you,' she said, and felt the warmth of a blush light her face. But she'd needed to say it, to make sure that he knew why she had hugged him—as a token of gratitude, nothing else. The physical effect the seemingly innocent gesture had awakened was merely an unforeseen consequence.

'It's the least I can do,' he replied in a gravelly voice, and she knew that their contact had affected him, too.

What was more surprising to her was that he looked as though he genuinely meant the words, that he wasn't just saying them automatically.

She cleared her throat. 'So...we should probably start rallying the troops.'

He nodded his agreement, and she forced herself to shift focus. She could be professional. She prided herself on it, in fact. She began to explain her strategy—she would speak to the vendors first, since they knew her, and then introduce them to Jordan as the new owner of the vineyard. Then they would pitch their event, find out if they were interested and available, and hope for the best. Since the will stipulated that they should give evidence of trying their best to find exactly the same service providers for the event, she would record their interactions and use them to show Mark if they needed to find alternatives.

'You've thought of everything, haven't you?'

'That's the job,' she replied, her neck prickling at the admiration she heard in Jordan's voice.

'Where have I heard *that* before?' he muttered, and she remembered she'd said something similar to him the first time they'd met.

She brushed off the nostalgia. 'We'd better get to it.'

They spent almost two hours there. It was time spent waiting for vendors to find a moment to talk to them in between serving people, and eating to fill that time. She found herself growing more comfortable as the minutes went by, the tension that was always inside her around him easing.

He was a wonderful ambassador for the vineyard, she thought as she watched him, and even though all the vendors remembered her and their event—especially since she had used many of them multiple times before—it was Jordan they responded to. He spoke to them with such warmth, with such praise, that she could almost see their spines straighten with pride. He played up his enjoyment of their food so much that sometimes she found herself giggling.

The sound was strange, even to her, and she wondered why it was so easy to relax around him now. Her determination to focus on the event and ignore whatever was between them had been decided just that morning. A few hours later and she had spoken to him about the past, made herself

vulnerable by admitting that she hadn't thought
she was worthy of him, and had walked down an
intimidating staircase. And now she was laughing with him. *At* him.

She knew that at some point he had gone from
entertaining the vendors to trying to make *her*
laugh. She wasn't sure how she felt about that,
but she chose not to ponder it then. Not when for
the first time in a long time she felt...free.

'Ice cream?'

She looked at him when she heard his voice,
and realised that she had been staring off into
space while she thought about the day.

'I'm not sure it's warm enough for ice cream,'
she replied, feeling self-conscious now.

'The sun is shining, Mila. We should thank it
by offering it the traditional food of appreciation.'

Her lips curved. 'And that's ice cream?'

'Yes, it is.' He smiled back at her and her heart
thumped. It was as if they were on a first date, she
thought, and then immediately cast the thought
aside.

'Besides, we have one more vendor to see,' he
continued, 'and he still hasn't returned from his
supply run.'

She shrugged off her hesitation. 'Sure—okay.'

She followed him to the ice-cream stand, where they joined a long line.

'Seems like everyone wants to make a sacrifice to the gods,' she said, and smiled at him when he looked at her.

'I told you so,' he replied, and took her hand as though it was the most natural thing in the world.

And the truth was that on that day, after talking, after laughing together, with the winter sun shining on their faces, holding hands *did* seem natural. But it wasn't, she reminded herself, and let go of his hand under the guise of looking for the notepad where she had written down the names of all the vendors and made notes.

'I think we've done pretty well today,' she said, and pretended not to notice the disappointment that had flashed across his face. 'Of the six vendors here, three are interested and are available for two weeks—the end of this month and the beginning of next. It cuts our time in half. Not ideal, but I think it's doable. And if we speak to the owner of the Bacon Bites food truck when he gets back, we could have four.'

'So that means we only have to replace two or three?'

Jordan slipped his hands into the pockets of his jacket, and she wondered if it was because he was tempted to take her hand again.

Her hand itched at the thought.

'Yes, but we still need to hear from two vendors who aren't here. Lulu said she would follow up on those. But I think we could substitute any who don't come with some of the other vendors here. I chatted to the woman who owns the chocolate truck over there—' she gestured to it with her head '—and she thought our event sounded great. She told me to come over if we were interested.'

'How did you manage to speak to her?'

'Oh, it was between your moan of delight for the meat pies and your groan of appreciation for the burger sliders,' she teased, and saw the tension that had entered his body after she'd let go of his hand fade.

'They have good food here,' he said, with a shrug and a smile.

Before she could respond they were at the front of the line. Behind the glass casing of the van she could see a variety of ice cream flavours that made her mouth water. After a few minutes of looking, she still couldn't decide between the chocolate hazelnut flavour and the vanilla toffee.

'How about you take the chocolate hazelnut and I take the vanilla toffee?' he said when she told him as much, and she smiled at the proposal. 'Perfect!'

She relayed their order to the patient vendor, and watched with delight at he made the sugar cone their ice cream would be served in from scratch.

Her first lick was deliciously creamy, and the thrill of cold ran down her spine. But then she realised that Jordan was watching her—with amusement and something else in his eyes— and she wondered if the thrill *had* come from the cold.

'This is great,' she said to avoid feeling awkward. 'Want some?'

'Sure,' he replied, and moved closer.

He watched her as he tasted the ice cream, and suddenly it was a year ago, when they'd been on honeymoon in Mauritius and had come across an ice-cream stand. It had been perfect for the hot summer's day after they'd been at the beach all morning.

Sharing their ice creams with one another had been...*sensual,* she thought, just as it was now. Shivers went up her spine at the look in his eyes—the look that told her that even though they weren't together any more he still wanted her.

He offered her a lick of his, and as though she was in a trance she leaned forward and tasted it, her eyes still on his. The flavour was just as delectable as she'd thought it would be, but the thought barely registered. Instead she was wondering if their sharing ice cream would end the way it had in Mauritius—with a passion that could have heated the entire resort for a week.

The thought had her moving backwards so quickly she almost stumbled. She regained her balance in time to realise that there was ice cream on her nose. She spent a few seconds trying to figure out how to remove it, and sighed when she saw that neither of them had taken a serviette.

'Do you want some help?' he asked, and she looked up to see that he was watching her—again—this time with an amused expression. And then she thought that she must have been crossing her eyes to look at the spot of ice cream on her nose, and she flushed.

'No, thanks—I'll manage.' She rubbed her nose with her sleeve and quickly turned to look for the vendor they were waiting for, hoping with all her might that he would be there. Relief swamped her when she saw that he was, and she turned back to Jordan, who was now watching her with a guarded expression.

'We should go over there,' she said, and gestured behind her.

He nodded and started walking, and she took a moment to instruct her emotions to stop fluttering around and get into place. When she was sure she had them under control she followed him—and wished with all her might that the roller coaster the two of them were on would stop.

CHAPTER TEN

'WHERE ARE WE GOING?'

They were in the car and supposed to be heading home from the school. But after spending the entire day with Mila, Jordan didn't want it to end.

Yes, they lived together at the moment—he kept waiting for her to tell him she would be leaving—but as soon as they walked through the front door of his father's house Jordan knew that Mila would erect a fence between them. He would be able to see glimpses of her, but he wouldn't be able to get near her, and the thought of that disturbed him.

He didn't think about why—he didn't need to defend himself for the time he spent with the woman who had once been his everything, did he?—but he couldn't bear being kept at a distance any more. Not after he'd seen parts of her today that he hadn't known existed during their marriage.

And now he knew what he had been missing.

'Did you know the Gerbers?'

'The old couple who used to live behind us?'

Mila turned to him, her brows drawn together in a frown, and Jordan's hand itched to reach out and smooth it over. But he tightened his hands on the steering wheel. Just as he had tightened them into fists in his pockets to keep himself from taking her hand again that afternoon.

He had done that by mistake, but it had felt so right that he hadn't let go even though his mind had told him to. And then she had done it instead, and disappointment had hit him like water from a burst pipe. He blamed that desire to touch her on that hug she'd sprung on him after making it down those stairs.

His body awoke just at the thought of it.

'Yeah...' He forced himself to speak, forced his body to calm down. 'Did you ever speak to them? Get a look around their property?'

'I... No,' she said, confusion clear in her voice. 'What's going on, Jordan? Where are you taking me?'

He had wanted to keep it a surprise, but he didn't want her to worry. 'I'm taking you to our house.'

'What?'

Was that panic her heard in her voice?

He frowned. 'Is something wrong?'

'No, no,' she replied quickly—too quickly—and looked out of the window. Her hands were clasped so tightly together in her lap that he reached over with one of his.

'What's going on, Mila?'

She blew out a shaky breath and he felt the deliberate relaxation of her hands under his. Taking it as a sign that she didn't want to be touched, Jordan moved his hand away. Even that slight loss of contact made him feel empty.

'It's nothing.'

'Mila…' Again, he found himself pleading.

She sighed. 'I just haven't been there since… since you left.'

'And going back now is…worrying for you?'

She didn't answer, and he glanced over to see her deliberately relaxing again. It made him wonder about why she was reacting this way to something as simple as going back to the house they'd shared. He felt a slight stir in his brain and frowned. He was missing something.

'A reminder of the past,' she finally said softly,

and when he looked at her again he saw that she was still looking out of the window. 'Going back to the house we lived in... Going back together... It's just a reminder of a life that seems worlds away.'

'We were planning to go anyway, weren't we? I have to help you get the stuff out so that you can leave.' Even saying the words sent a flash of pain through his heart.

'Oh, yes, of course,' she said, again more quickly than he thought she needed to, and again he wondered what he was missing.

There had to be something... The stirring in his brain seemed like a distant memory, but he couldn't recall it to verify whether that was the truth, and he didn't know if it had anything to do with what was currently happening between them. But it must—why else did he feel as if he was having a conversation without knowing all the facts?

'It's probably because this is unplanned,' she continued. 'Why are we going there now?'

'I have something to show you,' he replied, forcing himself to ignore the dull thud of unrecalled memories and focus on what his intention had been from the beginning. 'Did you ever see that pathway in the backyard, just next to that huge tree we planned to turn into a tree house for the little grape?'

He heard her sharp intake of breath before he realised he had used the pet name they had given their child after finding out they were having a boy. They had been so happy, he thought, pain tainting the memory. It had been the first time they had considered names for the baby, and he had teased her, calling him 'the little grape' since their child would one day have to take over the vineyard.

Mila had protested, of course, and with each objection had come a splutter of laughter that had warmed Jordan's insides so much that the name had stuck. They'd had a list of real names, of course, but they had never got the chance to decide on what they would call him.

'Yes, I remember,' she said hoarsely, and he reached for her hand, not caring about the unspoken rules that meant he shouldn't.

'I'm sorry, Mila, I didn't mean to—'

'It's okay.' She squeezed his hand. 'I think it's time we weren't afraid to refer to our son.'

He tightened his hand on hers and then let go, unable to keep the contact. His son was always in his thoughts—and always would be. He couldn't escape the way it had felt to hold his dying son in his arms when he'd been barely big enough to fit in Jordan's hands.

But she was right—he *had* been afraid to speak about him. And there was a lot more to it than just the fact that he couldn't bring himself to do it. No, admitting to Mila earlier that he'd been scared when they'd found out she was pregnant was only the tip of the iceberg. It hadn't fully left his mind since their conversation, and he'd realised that, as he'd initially thought, he *had* been scared he would turn out to be the same as his father. And that *was* part of the reason he'd left for Johannesburg.

Jordan knew Greg had loved him, but his childhood had been tainted by his father's grief. Grief that had made Greg into a bitter and sometimes angry man. The years after his mother had died had been filled with tension for Jordan—he'd sometimes felt as if he was walking on eggshells when he was around Greg. As a child, Jordan hadn't understood why his father would never look at him in the eye, or why Greg had spoken *at* him instead of *to* him. If he'd ever spoken to Jordan at all.

He had started behaving badly because of it, which had strained his relationship with Greg even more. It had also led to the night that would be burned in his memory for ever. The night that had changed Jordan—and his father—with only a few words.

Jordan vaguely remembered a time when laughing had been easy for his father. When there had been an open affection between them. But those memories were so faded he wondered if he'd made them up. The memories that were clear were of a steady man—a sombre, reserved and often difficult man. It clearly highlighted the fact that when Jordan had lost his mother, he'd lost his father, as well. And that had led to Jordan not being able to grieve fully for his mother because, frankly, his father had done it for both of them.

He hadn't thought about it until Mila had told him she was pregnant, and then suddenly he'd spent nights worrying about whether that grief for his mother would pop up once Mila had had the baby. Whether that grief would turn him into the kind of angry man his father was and spoil his son's childhood *and* Jordan's marriage.

It had made him worry that they'd rushed into marriage, made him think that he should have considered those possibilities when he'd been able to do something about them.

And when they'd lost the baby his fears had only intensified. He'd lost someone he loved, just as his father had, which surely upped the chances of Jordan turning into Greg. So Jordan had left. Escaped. Or, as he'd recently realised, run away…

'He's not alone, you know,' Mila said suddenly as he pulled into the driveway of their old house. 'The little grape's with our parents.'

He glanced over and saw a tiny smile on her lips. It made her look peaceful, he thought, and a large part inside him settled at the thought. It brought *him* peace, too.

'That's a really lovely thing to think about, isn't it?'

She smiled at him, and something in his heart eased. Was that because she'd smiled at him—a sweet, genuine smile that he had only been privy to that day—or was it because it comforted him to think about two generations of his family together?

'He'll have met your mom,' Mila said softly. 'I always wished I could have met her, you know. Your father used to talk about her sometimes.'

Jordan could tell that Mila was looking at him, but he stared steadily ahead. He didn't want to talk about his mother. That would mean telling her about his father. About his childhood. About his fears.

'She sounded amazing.'

He didn't respond, and then he tilted his head. 'Come on. Before it gets dark.'

He got out of the car, aware of the disappointment that shrouded her, and waited for her to join him as he stood outside the house they'd lived in during their short marriage. The first time he had seen the house he had thought it timeless and elegant—exactly what he had been looking for for his sweet, beautiful bride.

A marble pathway led to large oak doors that looked newly polished yet still antiquated. Large glass windows overlooked the road, and gave the white façade a modern feel. The pathway was lined with palm trees, which had always made him feel as if he was walking into an oasis of some kind. It still looked the same to him now, though all the memories made him feel more than he had the first time he had seen it.

Now he thought about those days when they'd had breakfast on the patio, just as the sun went up. She had always moaned about getting up that early, but the peace on her face when she was curled up on a chair, a cup of coffee in her hand, made him think she'd thought it worth it. He remembered walking hand in hand with her through their garden, where the roses that were planted there were always the perfect gift for her. And he could still see her lying next to the pool, the slight swell of her stomach obvious in her swimming costume. Could still feel the surge of protectiveness that had gone through him when he'd looked at her.

'It looks the same...but it feels different,' she said beside him, and he looked down at her to see a mixture of emotions playing over her face that had him grabbing for her hand.

He could feel that she was shaking, and just like that he realised what he'd been missing in the car—why she'd been anxious about coming back.

'It reminds you of your fall, doesn't it?'

She didn't have to answer him—he could see the truth of his words on her face.

I'm an idiot, he thought, and wondered how he hadn't thought about it before.

His mind had been too focused on showing her the secret he'd kept since he'd found out that she was pregnant. He hadn't wanted today to end, hadn't wanted her guard to come up, and in the process his actions to prevent it had hurt her.

He was a selfish man, he thought in disgust.

'I sometimes still dream about it,' she said quietly, and he immediately wanted to hold her in his arms.

But her words told him that she was forcing herself to face it—it was that fire he'd noticed in her when he'd returned again—and he told himself to be content with holding her hand.

'I can feel myself falling, reaching for a railing that wasn't there for support. And then the impact of rolling down the stairs.' She drew a shaky breath. 'I still feel foolish for falling down five steps.'

'It had been raining,' he said immediately,

his heart clenching in pain at the anguish—the guilt—that he heard in her voice.

She ignored him. 'I lay there, my breath gone, with shock keeping me from feeling the true pain of what my body had just gone through, and I felt warmth between my legs and realised...'

Her hand was so tight on his that he could tell there was no blood flowing through it, but that didn't matter to him. Not when he could feel the pain of what she had gone through—what she had never spoken of before. Not when he could hear the quickness of her breath. He drew her in, though she didn't seem to notice.

'I realised that something was wrong...that I had done something wrong...and then I saw you, and your face told me that I was right.'

Tears fell from her eyes and he didn't care this time if he was interrupting her. His arms went around her and she sobbed—heart-wrenching sobs that broke everything inside him each time he heard them.

'I'm sorry, Jordan. I'm sorry I wasn't more careful. I'm sorry I didn't slow down like you asked me to. I'm sorry I didn't look after him like I should have.'

'You didn't do anything wrong, Mila.' He felt his own tears as he said the words. 'I shouldn't have asked you to slow down. It was just…fear. My own. I think I was hoping to slow *us* down.' He paused, held her tightly. 'Everything was happening so quickly.'

He could feel her body shake, knew his words weren't having any effect. So he told her the facts, hoping their simplicity would help her.

'You were walking down stairs we'd both used a million times before. It had been raining—a light summer rain that had come from nowhere. You slipped. It was an accident.'

He said the words over and over again—to himself just as much as to her—until her shaking dissipated and everything went still. They stood in each other's arms longer than was necessary, their grief finally—*finally*—something they shared.

Not completely, a voice reminded him, and he stepped back. His heart thudded painfully in his chest as a reminder of what he needed to tell her—worse now that he knew about the guilt she felt. And the expression on her face—the com-

pletely exhausted expression—tempted him to
ignore it, to tell her some other time.

But he knew that was just an excuse. He
wouldn't ever get to that other time—not when
he had been meaning to tell her since the accident. And now she had bared her soul to him he
knew he couldn't keep it a secret from her any
more.

'There's something I need to tell you.' He said
it quickly, afraid that he wouldn't get through it
otherwise. 'I had to give them permission to operate on you, Mila. You were bleeding from the
abruption, losing consciousness...'

He shook his head.

'Waiting for the bleeding to subside would have
put you *and* the baby at risk.' He took a shaky
breath, not daring to look at her—not yet. 'I had
to approve the C-section knowing there was a
chance our baby wouldn't survive. But I couldn't
take a chance on losing both of you...'

His voice had gone completely hoarse at this
admission of something he had carried with him
for what felt like for ever, and he forced himself
to look at her before he lost his courage. She was
staring at him, those eyes more haunting than

ever before, carefully blank of all the emotion he wished he could read in her.

Her hand reached up, and he braced himself for the pain of a slap, but she only brushed away the remnants of her tears from her cheeks. Then she cleared her throat.

'I know.'

He looked at her, his eyes wide. 'What?'

'The doctor told me when I went back for my check-up. And then I asked Greg about it and he confirmed it.'

'Your check-up was…' He sorted through the memories 'I was still here, Mila… Why didn't you tell me you knew?' He couldn't believe that the burden he had been carrying with him for such a long time wasn't a secret after all.

'I was waiting for *you* to tell me.'

The look she aimed at him made him feel like a schoolboy.

'I wanted to, but I was afraid—'

'That I would blame you for it?'

He nodded, and she folded her arms.

'I did. I thought it was your fault that I didn't get to see my son alive. Why do you think I asked for space?'

He was dumbfounded, the words of apology, of excuse, he'd prepared were wiped from his mind.

'I thought you would go and stay with your dad for a while, and I would be able to deal with all the feelings. I was raw, hurting and in more pain than I thought possible. I just needed time.'

She looked at him, and he saw her anger.

'But then you left me completely. And instead of space I got divorce papers.'

'You're angry with me…' But he'd known that, he thought. Deserved it.

'Yes, I am. But not about you giving them permission to operate. What choice did you have?' She shook her head. 'We both might not have survived if you hadn't.' She paused, kicked at a stone. 'I *was* angry about it. But only because I wished I could have held him during those seventeen minutes he was alive.'

Her breath caught at that, and Jordan wished he could hold her again.

'And then I thought that if it couldn't be me— and since I was still under anaesthesia then it couldn't have been—you were the only other person I would have wanted it to be. So after a while I forgave you.' She looked at him stonily. 'It wasn't your fault either, Jordan.'

'I can't believe you've known all along. I've been carrying this with me ever since I...' He trailed off when he saw her jaw set and she looked away. And then he realised that she'd said that she wasn't angry with him about *that* any more. 'Why *are* you angry at me, then?'

'You really don't know?'

He opened his mouth to answer, but she waved him away.

'If you can't figure it out then you don't deserve to know.' She set her jaw. 'Can we just leave now, please?'

'No, we can't.' He felt uncomfortable, but he said it because he'd shared one of his deepest secrets with her, which he wouldn't have done with anyone else, and now she was pulling away. Even though he didn't want to delve any further into emotion—his insides were raw and knotted from what had already been said—he persisted. 'I want you to tell me what else I've done wrong.'

'So you can continue with this victim mentality you seem to have going?'

Anger sparked, deep inside him, and pumped through his body with his blood. 'Excuse me?'

'Every tragedy that's happened to you, you somehow blame yourself for it.'

He could see the anger in her, too, but that only fuelled his own.

'You blame yourself for approving an operation that saved my life—that gave your son his best chance at living—and you blame yourself for your father's death. Oh, did you think I couldn't see the weight of guilt crushing you?'

He kept his face clear of the turmoil he felt— the anger and truth in her words were daggers piercing his insides—and wondered how she had realised what he felt about his father's death.

'You think that his heart attacks were because you left. Because you didn't keep in touch over the past year. You hate it that he died without fixing whatever was wrong between you.'

'Stop!' he said, his hands clenched into fists at his sides.

'Why?' she demanded, her face flushed from her tirade. '*You* were the one who wanted me to continue, remember?' She didn't wait for his affirmation before continuing, as though she was purging herself of everything that she felt. 'Do you want to know what I'm *really* angry about, Jordan? It's because you ran away when I needed you the most.' She took a shaky breath. 'You made me feel like you left because I had lost our child.'

She was trembling, and he itched to touch her, to comfort her, even as her words shook him. 'Stop saying that! Stop blaming yourself for what happened. It wasn't your fault.' And she'd made him see that it wasn't his either.

'If that's not the reason, then why did you go?'

'I was running—just like you said,' he shot out, and immediately stilled.

'Why?'

'Does it matter?' he said, exasperated. He couldn't deal with the emotion any more. 'I'm back now.'

Her eyes flashed. 'Yes, it *matters*, Jordan. And here's why.'

She grabbed the front of his top, and before he knew it her lips were on his.

CHAPTER ELEVEN

SHE'D DONE IT out of desperation, to pierce through that controlled façade he clung to even though she could see that he felt beneath the surface. She wanted him to feel the earthquake that was happening inside her, to know the emotions that sprang from the hole the quake had opened, and the only way she knew how to do that was to kiss him.

But as she sank into the kiss she thought that she was a fool for being so impulsive, for letting go of the control she'd fought for around him. And then she stopped thinking, pressing her body closer to his as she tasted him.

The same...he tasted the same. Of fire and home and pure man.

Her anger had turned into passion, so there was no gentle sliding back into the heat they had always shared. No, they jumped straight into the fire, greedily taking each other, their hands mov-

ing over bodies that had changed yet were somehow still the same.

When he lifted her from the ground she went
willingly, her arms around him, refusing to lose
contact with him. She barely felt the wall that
he pressed her against, her senses captivated by
what his hands were doing. He pushed aside the
jacket she had on, his tongue playing with hers
in a way that had her moaning, and the sound
seemed to burn away the last of his patience with
her clothing.

He ripped open the shirt she wore, his hands
roaming over her bare skin before she even heard
the buttons fall on the marble path to their home.
Though the house was enclosed, and there was
no one who would see them, Mila didn't think
she would have cared if there had been. Her body
was too occupied in being touched by the hands
that had always owned it, her mind too employed
by the pleasure only he could make her feel.

She fumbled with his clothes, wanting to touch
his skin as he did hers. Giving up, she slid her
hands under his top and eagerly over his body.
The toned, muscular body that she had wanted
since the moment she had seen him. Somewhere

she thought about how different touching him felt now, but the thought was vague, dulled by the passion of his lips on her skin.

She wanted him, she heard her heart tell her as he kissed her neck, letting her head fall back to give him better access. And she would have let him have her, she thought later, had her phone not rung.

The sound was muffled, since the phone was in her jacket pocket, but it was clear enough to give them both pause. And the pause allowed her thoughts to spin back into her mind.

Though most were still muddled and hazy, one came to her with the clarity of a conscience after confession—she was giving herself to the man who had broken her heart. And one more occurred to her after that—he was still breaking it.

She pushed him away, ignoring the desire that clouded his face, and with one hand held her torn shirt together. She walked a short distance away from him, took a deep breath and answered her phone.

The conversation only lasted a few minutes, but it was enough for her thoughts to clear and her cheeks to flush with embarrassment. She was a fool! she thought, keeping the phone at her ear even though Simon, Karen's manager, had long since said goodbye. Why had she thought *kissing* him would make him *feel*? The only thing it had done was to awaken her body and alert her mind to the fact that she was still alive. That she was still a woman who needed, who *wanted*. And that both those needs and wants had to do with Jordan.

She shoved the phone back into her pocket, and zipped up her jacket, not wanting to feel any more exposed than she already did.

'Who was that?'

She turned at his voice, hating it that she still remembered the effect it had had on her the day they had met. That it still had an effect now.

'Karen's manager.' Mila didn't look at him, not wanting him to see the emotions she couldn't hide nearly as well as he did. 'She's doing a show at the university's conservatorium tonight. She wants us to come through.'

There was a moment that beat between them, and then he asked, 'What kind of show does a pop star do at a *conservatorium*?'

'A performance for her studies, apparently,' she

answered him. 'It's formal, and it starts in an hour and a half. We'd better get going.'

She strode past him, determined not to look at him, and braced herself for contact when out of the corner of her eye she saw his hand lift. But the contact never came and she sighed with relief—*not* disappointment, she assured herself— and got into the car.

It was going to be a long trip home.

Mila stood under the shower, angling her head so that the warm water could hit her body directly. She stayed like that, hoping that it would wash away her actions of that day. She cringed every time she thought about it, and the day wasn't even over yet. Now, after nearly tearing Jordan's clothes off, Mila was going to have to spend who knew how long with him at a classical concert by the winner of a pop competition.

There was no way around it, she thought, shampooing her hair. Simon had told her that Karen wanted to speak to her before making a decision about the event, and this was the only time she could spare to do it.

At least it meant that Mila wouldn't have to go

to a teenybopper concert with Jordan. She could only imagine how the girls would swoon around him. Hadn't she just had first-hand experience of that? Her body still trembled from his touch, reminding her of how good that part of their relationship had been. But what good did that do when there were other, more substantial cracks between them?

Mila knew she had made progress with him, getting him to admit that he'd had to give permission for her C-section. But at what cost? He now knew more about her than she'd wanted him to know—he knew she didn't want to go back to the house, that it reminded her of the accident. He knew that she still dreamt about it, and that she was angry at him for leaving. It was a miracle that he'd admitted that he'd run away, but she still couldn't get him to tell her why. She couldn't even get him to talk about his mother.

Everything was so *controlled* with him. Sometimes she wondered where the man who had given her a surprise picnic the day they had met had gone. That impulsive, romantic man who had swept her off her feet and convinced her to marry him. He didn't seem to exist any more, she thought, and got out of the shower. No, he had been replaced by the man who had run away when she'd needed him—the man who never wanted to speak to her about the things that mattered.

And still the man who set her body on fire.

Calm down, she instructed herself. She just needed to get through the event and then she would be moving on with her life, away from Jordan and all the problems he created for her. And to do that she needed to get Karen to set a date so that things could finally move ahead.

Mila would ignore the voice in her head that told her that finding out what Jordan didn't want to tell her was about more than just her. The voice that told her Jordan needed to admit it to himself, too, or he would carry the guilt of his past for the rest of his life. It might have been harsh, but she had meant it when she'd referred to him seeing himself as a victim.

It wasn't her problem, she reminded herself. And even if finding out would mean she would have to sacrifice a part of herself that she had carried for a long time, there was part of her that didn't want to ask for what she wanted. That couldn't. There was no way Mila would do that when there was nothing on the line—no relationship, no family—and she had no guarantee Jordan would do the same for her.

So she focused on getting ready. She took out the only two dresses she had kept when she'd moved in with Greg that were formal enough to work for the event. One was a knee-length loose black dress. Pretty enough to wear to a formal event, but demure enough not to draw attention.

She put it in front of her body and realised that it was no longer something she wanted to wear. It reminded her of someone she no longer seemed to be, and she took a moment to figure out whether she was okay with that. When the thought didn't make her feel anxious something settled inside her, and she pressed her hand to her stomach with a small smile.

Maybe she was changing for the better, she thought, and then put the thought away as something she would take with her when she moved on. And when *that* thought unsettled her she dismissed it completely and looked at the second dress.

It was long and midnight blue, with a lace

halter-neck overlay that led down her arms to form sleeves. It covered the sweetheart neckline designed to show off her bust, and though she would have preferred something *completely* covered after her actions earlier, she put the dress on and chose to feel confident in it. *Another change?* she considered.

She fluffed her hair, sighing when her curls wouldn't play along, and decided to leave it loose. She might as well accept all of herself, she thought, and spent a few minutes on make-up. She looked in the mirror when she was done, told herself to be careful around Jordan, and then grabbed her purse and headed for the front door.

Jordan was already there, and her heart screamed in protest at how handsome he looked. He was wearing a tuxedo that showed off his strong body and looked as if it had been designed to make her breath catch. He had shaved—the five o'clock shadow that had brushed her skin earlier was only a memory now—and had smoothed back his hair, and he looked at her with an unreadable expression that reminded her of a celebrity who was preparing to walk the red carpet.

But as his eyes swept over her his expression

slipped enough for her to see his appreciation of her outfit, and she blushed.

'You're wearing your hair down,' he said.

'Yes, I am,' she answered, and resisted the urge to fiddle with it.

'That's the way I remember it.'

Her heart rapped in her chest, like someone desperately knocking at a door, and she forced herself to calm down. What did it matter if that was how he remembered it?

'It's the way I like it,' he said softly, as though he had been privy to her thoughts, and she had to fight against the embarrassment.

'Are you ready to go?' she said, instead of responding to his comment, and almost turned away from him before she saw the look in his eyes.

Gooseflesh immediately shot out on her skin, and she resisted the urge to pull at the material around her neck to get more air. He was looking at her as though he would have liked to continue from where they had left off earlier, and his eyes pierced her right down to her soul.

After a moment his face went back to being unreadable, and she sighed in relief and grabbed her coat from the rack that stood behind the front door.

Jordan opened the car door for her when they reached it, and she carefully got in, trying to avoid all contact with him. Which was in vain, she realised, when the train of her dress still lay outside her door after she'd sat down and they both reached to get it.

Their hands touched for the briefest moment, and yet the feeling reminded her of the way she had felt when she'd burned herself the day before. She snatched it back and let Jordan tuck her dress into the car, and only exhaled when he closed her door and walked around to get in at his side.

'Do you have *any* idea why a pop star would be studying classical music?'

He spoke without looking at her, and she wondered if he knew how tight his hands were on the steering wheel despite his outward calm.

'Your guess is as good as mine,' she murmured, proud of the aloof tone she had managed.

She made an extra effort not to fold her arms, which would, for sure, give away *her* nerves about spending time with him. Because, as much as she didn't want to be affected by him, she inevitably always was.

The rest of their journey was made in silence, and she tried not to use it as an opportunity to spend more time thinking about everything. Relief hit her right to her bones when the car stopped at the university's conservatorium. It was a large white building, with the word *conservatorium* printed boldly at the top, and the glass doors at the bottom were open to the crowds who, for some reason, were pouring into the venue.

She looked up in surprise when her door clicked open, and realised that the time she had spent ogling the building meant she'd been distracted from climbing out of the car by herself. Now she was faced with the hand Jordan was offering to help her out.

She couldn't say no, she thought, even if that had been her immediate reaction. He was offering an olive branch, she realised when she saw his face.

She braced herself for the contact, but in no way did it help when she took his hand. Heat and memories slid through her like a warm knife through butter, from the hand he now held to the top of her head and right down to her feet. She tightened her hand on his in response, saw the feeling mirrored on his face, and got out so that they wouldn't have to spend any more time touching.

Except the pavement they had parked on was not meant for high heels, and after she'd stumbled for the second time Jordan snaked an arm around her waist and pulled her closer. Her body immediately groaned in delight at the feel of him so close, and her mind was fogged by the intoxicating smell of his body wash and cologne.

She ignored the effects it had on her body and pulled her coat tighter around her, as though the action would somehow protect her. She pulled away from him the moment they were inside the building, ignoring the way her heart protested at the emptiness she felt immediately, and gave her coat to a man with an unnecessarily prudish expression on his face.

'Mila, I'm so glad that you made it!'

Mila turned at the familiar male voice, and opened her arms to return a hug when she saw it was Simon.

'I'm so glad that you invited us, Simon! We appreciate Karen taking the time to speak to us.'

She pulled back and smiled, and then her skin prickled and she realised that Jordan had joined them.

'You've never met my...' She'd been about to say *husband*, but that didn't seem right. 'You've never met Jordan, have you? He owns the vineyard where Karen performed at the event where we met. Jordan—Simon.'

They shook hands, and she noted the way Jordan's 'businessman' expression slid easily onto his face.

'I'm glad to see you both. Unfortunately Karen won't have time until after the performance to talk to you two, but can you come backstage immediately after and we'll discuss the event then?'

'Yes, of course,' Mila answered.

'Great! I've given your names to the guys at the door, so you can go straight through.' Simon brushed a kiss on Mila's cheek, nodded at Jordan and then moved on to whoever was behind them in the line.

'I suppose we can't sneak out now,' she whispered to Jordan as they walked towards the door.

She looked at his face when he didn't respond, and was treated to the stormy expression she had seen that first day after he had returned.

'What's wrong?' she asked, but there was only silence.

She sighed and pulled him out of the line they were standing in, not wanting to be overheard.

'Look, I know what happened this afternoon was...wasn't ideal...' she rolled her eyes at her description '...but this is work. This is why we're here. Can you put your feelings aside so we can do this?'

His expression grew darker, and she was about to launch into another lecture about keeping the event and their personal feelings separate when his face grew blank. He gave her a curt nod, and then extended his arm for her to hook hers onto. She hesitated for a moment and then slipped her arm through his. If he was going to put his feelings aside then so could she, she thought, and ignored the spread of warmth through her body at his touch.

CHAPTER TWELVE

'YOU'RE HEARING THE same thing I am, right?'
Jordan glanced over at Mila, and saw that her jaw had dropped. She nodded at his question, and then quickly closed her mouth.

'This is ridiculous,' she whispered back to him, her eyes still riveted on the stage. 'Why do they have her doing those awful pop songs when she can sing like this?'

He chuckled—more at Mila's reaction than at the fact that Karen-the-pop-star was actually Karen-with-the-most-incredibly-beautiful-classical-voice. She was standing alone in front of an orchestra, her usual red curls straightened into a sophisticated updo that, along with her green ballgown, made her look a lot older than she was. More mature, too, he thought—which was probably the point, though not entirely necessary. Not when each note sent a wave of appreciation through the audience.

'Maybe this is so that she won't *have* to do "awful pop songs" any more,' he responded, and received a death glare from a woman in front of him, who looked like the kind of woman who always shushed people.

It was effective, though, and he didn't speak again until Karen's performance was over. She had been one of many performers that night, all of them students who were singing as part of their evaluation for a degree. And, although he knew that was why Karen had been performing that night, he had expected the beauty of her voice almost as much as he had expected that kiss he and Mila had shared that afternoon.

He sighed when he realised that he was thinking about it yet again.

Though how could he not? an inner voice asked him, and his mind played back portions of it. Mila coming towards him with passion in her eyes...the feeling of her lips on his...the desire that had shot through him and had him tearing at her clothes—literally—just about ready to take her against the wall of the house they had once shared...

If she hadn't taken that phone call he wasn't

sure he would have been able to help himself, although he definitely should have...

He wasn't sure if he was grateful for that call or annoyed by it.

Since his mind kept slipping back to that afternoon, he was grateful when all the performances were over and they could make their way backstage. Jordan saw Simon standing with Karen, and warned himself against the jealousy that still threatened. When he'd met Simon, Jordan had noted the easiness of the interaction between him and Mila. He'd only vaguely been able to remember a time when things had been that easy between himself and Mila—when they'd been married, probably—and that thought had led to the annoyance that Mila had incorrectly interpreted as anger earlier.

But Jordan had shaken it off now, and he forced himself to remember that as Simon waved them over.

'Karen, I can't believe it was you out there!' Mila pulled the smiling girl in for a hug. 'It can't be only two years since that event. You have grown up *so* much since then!'

'It makes a huge difference when I'm not in

leather tights singing about boys breaking my heart, doesn't it?' Karen responded, and Mila laughed.

'Yeah—although I can't disregard the value of the tights *or* the songs. They're the reason we're able to see *this* amazing side of you.'

It still impressed Jordan to see how good Mila was at networking, even though he'd spent the afternoon witnessing it. She had made every vendor feel as though they were her friend, he remembered, asking them about details of their lives that he was sure they had only mentioned to her in passing. And then, when they had been buttered up by the personal conversation, she would segue into the professional.

Now she was complimenting Karen on her current performance but still highlighting their need for the other side of her to perform. It wasn't only a testament to how good she was at networking, he realised suddenly, it was smart, too.

'They're the reason she's here, too,' Simon chimed in. 'Some well-placed donations helped her get in, even though she had missed the application deadline.'

Mila smiled at Simon, though Jordan saw the

flash of annoyance in her eyes, and he found himself agreeing. Why would Karen's manager undermine her talent like that?

'I'm sure it didn't take that much convincing with your voice, though,' Mila said smoothly, and Jordan felt warmth radiate from the smile Karen aimed at Mila.

She cared, he thought, though he wasn't sure why he hadn't thought about that before. Since he'd come back Jordan had learned all kinds of things about his wife—and was clearly still learning. He knew more than he'd known before. She was feisty, and he was beginning to realise just how much he liked it. It made her a lot more confident, he thought as he watched it first-hand and felt the tug of attraction.

'Oh, I'm sorry!' Mila turned to him and he re- alised it was his turn to perform. 'I don't think you met Jordan the night of the first Under the Stars event, did you?'

'No, I didn't.'

Karen held out her hand, and Jordan smiled at the interest he saw coming from her. She didn't try to hide it, which amused him even more. It seemed she'd grown up a lot from the whiny teen who'd cried at a broken heart, he thought.

'It's lovely to meet you, Karen. Mila was absolutely right about that performance. If you don't get an A for that, then I'm not sure the lecturers were listening properly.'

'How very kind of you to say, Jordan.'

He hid a smile at the flirtatious tone of her voice.

'Simon tells me that you're interested in me performing at an event you're hosting at the vineyard?'

'Yeah, Mila and I are hosting it, actually.'

'You mean she's hosting the event *for* you?' Karen's eyes didn't leave his face.

'No, I mean we're hosting it together.'

Karen didn't know they were married, Jordan thought, and wondered how it would change things if he told Karen they were.

But then he saw the slight shake of Mila's head and continued, 'My father grew quite fond of Mila after the last event, and his dying wish was that we plan one more event in his name.'

It wasn't exactly a lie, was it?

'He essentially requested a replica of the event

you performed at a couple of years ago, in fact. Said he couldn't remember hearing someone sing as beautifully as you.' That, he thought, *was* an outright lie. But desperate times called for desperate measures.

'Oh, wow...' Karen breathed, and Jordan realised his earlier assumption hadn't been entirely correct.

She was still a teenager—she had just learned to hide it better.

'Well, I can't see myself saying no to such an amazing offer. I have time towards the end of the year, right, Simon?'

'Actually...' Mila interrupted whatever answer Simon had been about to give '... I mentioned to Simon that the concert will have to happen quite soon. Like before the end of next month.'

Karen frowned. 'Why so soon?'

Mila exchanged a look with Jordan that screamed "Help me!" and words came out of his mouth before he had an opportunity to think about them.

'Well, Mila's moving away at the end of next month to teach in Korea. She won't be able to do anything once she's gone, and I'd like to honour my father before she leaves, since we don't know when she'll be back.'

Mila bit her lip, and he could see she was trying to hide a smile.

'Yes, Karen—I'm going to teach English to little children in Korea, and I need to do this before I leave. Can you help?'

Karen looked at Simon. 'Tonight was my last exam, but I'll be going on tour in a few weeks and then I won't be available.'

'The proceeds will be going to charity,' Jordan said suddenly, inspired by his fear of losing Karen's performance and the repercussions that might have on their event. But now that he'd said it, he realised it wasn't a bad idea.

Mila raised her eyebrows at him, but said, 'An event for charity will have an awesome effect on your public image, Karen. And, Simon, I don't have to tell you how much that can do for Karen's tour.'

Simon waited a beat, and then whipped out his phone and tapped on the screen. 'She has a sold-out concert at Westgate Stadium this Saturday, but the following Saturday—the one before the tour—we don't have anything booked. It was intended to give her some rest before she leaves on tour. Would you be willing to sacrifice that?' Simon directed the question to Karen.

'Yeah, sure.' Karen turned to them in expectation, and all they could do was look at her with stunned expressions.

Mila was the first to recover.

'That's great. Would you mind helping us with the marketing, then? We'll organise the tickets, but support from you on social media will properly ensure that we have an audience for you. *And enough support for charity.*'

'Yeah, of course.' Karen's eyes shifted to someone behind them and she smiled. 'Look, you can chat to Simon about the arrangements—the set, details about soundcheck—and he'll let me know what the deal is. We can take it from there. I'm going to run. It was nice seeing you again, Mila... Jordan.'

Karen fluttered her eyelashes, and then walked over to join a group of giggling girls.

'I'll contact you tomorrow, when I've had more time to look at the schedule, and we can talk about things,' Simon said to them.

'Yeah, that's perfect. Thanks, Simon.'

Mila smiled at him, and Jordan nodded a farewell, his mind too consumed by what Mila had just got them into to be concerned about the interested look Simon threw at Mila as he walked away.

They stood in silence after Simon had left, and then Jordan gathered his wits to ask, 'Did you just agree to holding our event in two weeks' time?'

'I...I think I did,' Mila stammered, not quite believing that it was true. But her instincts had taken over, and the event planner inside her had jumped at the opportunity to secure a performer who would ensure their event was a success.

'What were you *thinking*?' he asked under his breath, and then gave a polite smile to the man who was returning their coats.

'I was thinking that we need Karen to make the event a success.'

'But you realise we don't actually need the event to be a success, right?'

He shot her a frown as he slid his coat on, and then turned for her to help him when his arm got stuck. Her hands shook a little, but she forced them to behave and helped him into the garment, lingering a tad too long at his shoulders.

'We just need there to *be* an event. Whether we have five or five hundred people there doesn't matter.'

'*You* were the one who said it was for charity,' she hissed at him. 'And you heard that she wouldn't be able to do it before our deadline otherwise. What was I supposed to do?'

'Find another performer?'

'It would have been more of an effort,' she replied, and he nodded as though he'd thought of that, too.

'You've made this much more difficult for us now,' he said stonily.

'I know that. But we both knew that this was a possibility when we spoke to the vendors today. It was either at the end of this month *with* Karen, or the beginning of next month without her.'

She was trying to convince herself as much as she was him, but suddenly she knew that she had done the right thing. That her actions would make the event a success. She really wanted it to be a success, she thought. And because she had just realised why, she said, 'It'll be the last thing

I do for Greg, Jordan. I want it to go as well as it possibly can.'

Her stomach knotted at her words. The intimacy of what she had revealed and the fact that she'd said it out loud warned her that she was growing too comfortable around Jordan. But up until that point it hadn't occurred to her that she might want to do the event for any reason other than the fact that she had to.

Now she knew she wanted to do it as a thank-you to Greg for all he had done for her—the last one she would be able to give him—and perhaps as a goodbye present to all those she cared about at the vineyard. A successful event would boost the vineyard's image and be a foundation they would be able to use to rebuild everything that had been put on pause over the last year with Greg's illness.

'I'm sorry, I—'

'No, it's fine,' she interrupted him, not wanting his sympathy.

She thanked the man for her coat, and took care to slip it on so that she wouldn't need Jordan's help as he had needed hers. They walked to the car in silence, though Jordan once again put an arm around her waist to keep her steady. She murmured a thank-you when she got into the car, and wondered why the silence was suddenly so bothersome. Maybe it was because she could feel, just beneath the armour she had put around her heart, her need for Jordan become stronger.

And he had only been back for three days.

That was another reason—one that also hadn't occurred to her until now—that she'd agreed to expedite the event. The quicker it happened, the sooner she would be able to get away from the reminder of a life that had never been hers to begin with. She would be free of all the wants and needs that were beyond her grasp, and she would finally be able to move on to a more real-istic future, where she would be safe from hurt...

'So, I'm going to teach in *Korea*?' she blurted out, sick of the direction of her thoughts.

Jordan chuckled, and the vibration of his voice sent a chill up her spine. Or maybe that was just the cold, she told herself desperately.

'One of the fellows at the research institute we started in Johannesburg told me about how his daughter was going to teach there in a few months. For some reason that was what jumped into my head when you sent me the fire signal for help.'

She smiled. 'Fire signal?'

'Your eyes were screaming "Help me!" so loudly I'm surprised no one else heard it.'

'I'm grateful that you came to my rescue—though now I'm wondering if Korea might be a good next step for me.'

She was still smiling, but her words reminded them that she would be leaving after the event. The thought was sobering—for both of them, she thought, when Jordan didn't respond—and again she sought for something to break the tension.

'How did things go with the institute?'

He looked over at her, and she wondered why he seemed to be checking to see if she was asking him seriously.

Because that's the excuse he used to leave the first time, she thought, and shook her head at the fact that everywhere she turned there was a reminder of a life she no longer had and a future that was uncertain.

'It went well,' he said after a moment. 'We had already started the ball rolling by then, so I just went there to finalise the staffing and ensure that the premises were suited for the expected capacity.'

'Was it?'

'Yeah, it was. It's in central Johannesburg, which is a great location, and it has enough space for the research fellows and for research seminars.'

'Worth the hassle of the accreditation process?'

She remembered the hours he'd had to spend on the phone, and the countless meetings when he'd first had the idea for a research institution for wine microbiology. He had wanted to give back—to contribute to the wine industry in some way other than just selling—and setting up an educational institution that would ensure the quality of the wines the Thomas Vineyard made as well as allow continued research into wine production had seemed like the way to do it. But getting accreditation from the Department of Education for some kind of qualification for the fellows had been a mission—as Jordan's facial expression now proved.

'Right now, with twenty fellows, I'm going to say yes.'

'Seems like you did a good thing, then.' She

meant it—though she wished it hadn't been at the expense of their relationship. But then again, they'd already established that that hadn't been the real reason—at least not the only one—that he'd left.

'How was living there?' she asked suddenly, thinking that perhaps knowing how Jordan had lived in his year without her would bring her some peace.

He frowned again, his hands still on the steering wheel, and she realised that they were already in front of the house. She waited a few more minutes and then shook her head in disappointment, feeling the cold run through her as she said, 'Don't tell me, then. I'll just add it to the list.'

She opened the car door, happy to escape from the desperate need inside her to know more about him. To know more about the aspects of his life that she hadn't been a part of.

To escape the need to demand to know about them.

'Mila, wait!' he called after her.

But she had already reached the front door and was trying to find her key to get in—to get away from him. The key fell from her hand, and she let out an exasperated breath as he came from behind her and picked it up.

He inserted the key into the door, but didn't turn it. 'I'll tell you,' he said, without looking at her, and she scoffed.

'I'm not pulling your teeth, Jordan. Talking to people is supposed to be natural. Or at least it's supposed to be with your *wife*.'

It was the first time she had referred to herself like that since learning that she *was* still his wife, and it sounded strange—maybe even terrifying—to hear it. But at the same time something came to rest inside her at the term—an acknowledgement of why learning about him had become so important.

She cared about him.

As a friend, she assured herself, not because she had been his wife. But even through her self-assurance she knew she was more hurt than she cared to admit that after all the revelations she'd made to him, he refused to share his own with her.

'I want to tell you,' he insisted. 'I want to talk to you… It's just difficult.'

Her eyebrows rose. 'Why?'

He exhaled sharply, and then turned the key in the lock. He pushed the door open and waited for her to walk through. When she had, she took her coat and hung it on the rack, then looked at him expectantly.

He would tell her this at least, she thought.

He took his jacket off, and then rubbed at his chin, which was already starting to show stubble. She remembered the slight burn on her skin from the friction earlier and her body responded with need.

To combat it, she folded her arms, and waited for him to speak.

'There's a lot I have to deal with. Since I came back here after Dad died...' He stuffed his hands into his pockets. 'It's hard for me to verbalise it. It's...a lot.'

She steeled herself against the softening that inevitably touched her heart, and said, 'We've both had to deal with "a lot," Jordan.' Her next words were already forming, and she ignored the voice telling her not to say them. 'Don't accuse me of pushing away the people who care about me when *you're* doing exactly the same thing.'

CHAPTER THIRTEEN

SHE HAD A POINT, Jordan thought, even as he wished for the old Mila. The one who would have understood him saying he had a lot to deal with and wouldn't have pushed. But hadn't he, only a few hours earlier, thought about how much he *liked* this new Mila? He couldn't change his mind now, just because she was making him uncomfortable. Especially when she was right.

'Fine—let's talk, then,' he forced himself to say, though he wasn't sure what he was prepared to talk about. 'But let me change first. I'd feel better in comfortable clothes.'

He wasn't sure how true that was, but he wasn't about to bare his soul in a tuxedo. Mila nodded, and he went to his bedroom, already unbuttoning his shirt.

The room hadn't changed much since his childhood, Jordan thought as he pulled on a pair of worn jeans and a long-sleeved shirt. It was still painted the blue his mother had chosen for him when he was younger. It had been one of their last activities together, before she had become too sick to get out of bed.

His memories of her had faded over time, but he still remembered how much time she had wanted to spend with him. He would play in front of the house on the patio, shouting for her to look when he did something that only a four-year-old would find impressive. And she had always sat on those chairs beside the front door, cheering for him, sharing his pride and telling him how happy he made her.

Even when his father had no longer joined her she'd sat there, watching over him. Even when she'd grown frailer, paler, more sickly, with his father hovering around, she'd spent hours with Jordan outdoors. His heart ached at the memories, which suddenly seemed so clear now, and he took a deep breath.

Why was he thinking about this *now*? There was no purpose in rehashing that part of his past. The part that reminded him of his father's anger towards him and, ever since he had learned the truth about his mother's death, his anger towards himself and the guilt he felt.

The thought had already put him on edge, and he forced himself to control it or he knew the conversation he was preparing to have with Mila could only go poorly.

It didn't work, since he found himself considering why he was preparing to have this conversation in the first place. Why had it all of a sudden become so important for her to see him trying? For her to see that he wanted to let her in, to tell her the real reasons behind why he had left?

There was no answer that would pull him away from the edge, and his insides tensed even further.

When he walked into the lounge, he noticed that she had started a fire. And then she walked into the room, a glass of wine in each hand, and his gut tightened.

She had changed, too, into a long-sleeved shirt he recognised as an old one of his. It was worn, and stretched so much that it almost touched her knees, which were clad in tights. She hadn't worn that particular shirt before, but it still reminded him of the times when she would wear his clothes. They smelled like him, she had always said, and he wondered if that was the reason she was wearing the shirt now.

The emotions that thought evoked—and his physical reaction to her—did nothing to make him feel better.

'How was my father before his death?' he asked abruptly, his voice harsher than he'd intended.

Her eyebrows rose in response, and he saw the flash of annoyance before it was replaced with ice.

Back to this again, he thought, but knew he was to blame for her reaction.

She set his glass down on the table in front of him, hard enough that he watched the contents swirl in disruption, and then she said, 'No, I'm not doing this with you when you're in this mood.'

'Mila, I don't have—'

'Whatever you're going to say, I'm sure I've heard it before. You don't feel like talking right now...or you're going through a lot...or can we postpone?' She shook her head. 'We don't have to have this conversation *at all*, Jordan.'

'No.' The word came quickly—something he

was sure was a result of the answers he hadn't wanted to consider earlier.

'Are you sure?' She raised her eyebrow, and her sassy look sent a shock of desire through him.

'Yes.'

Both brows rose now, and then she picked up her wine and settled back. 'We can start with something simple. Tell me about your life in Johannesburg.'

'There's not much to say. And I'm not saying that because I don't want to tell you,' he said quickly, when he saw the expression on her face. 'I spent most of my time at the institute. Too much time, probably. But it helped to focus on something other than...'

'Me,' she finished when he trailed off.

He nodded. 'And on everything else that had happened. I thought that if I could make a success of this, something I could actually control, then my failures at home...'

He was messing it up, he thought. Her finger was tracing the rim of her glass again, so although her face was unreadable he knew she was thinking about what he was saying. But he couldn't tell *what* she was thinking, and it was driving him crazy.

'I get that,' she said finally, and raised her eyes to look at him. 'When your dad got sick and asked me to move in…focusing on him instead of the things going on in my life helped me deal with everything.' She cocked her head. 'Did you have a social life?'

'You mean did I date?'

Her mouth opened slightly at the blunt question, and then she straightened her shoulders. 'I suppose so. Though I was talking about whether or not you had friends.'

His lips curved at the slight blush on her cheeks. But he answered her question,

'No dates, but I did go out for drinks with some of the people from work sometimes. Not often enough to keep in touch outside work now, though.'

She nodded, and sipped from her wine. It gave him a clear view of the line of her throat, and again he felt his need for her run through his blood with the memory of how he had kissed her there that afternoon.

'Can I ask about my father now?' he asked

quickly, before the need consumed him and he did something he regretted.

'Of course. What do you want to know?'

'Anything.'

Everything, he thought, but stopped the word before it came out.

'Well, he was devastated about the baby,' she began. 'Not that he would ever have said it. You know how he was.'

Yes, he did. And wasn't that part of why he was absorbing everything she was telling him now?

'I didn't speak to him that first month. Not to anyone, really, as you know. But he eventually told me he'd stayed away because he wanted us to deal with it together.'

Jordan remembered that. His father hadn't visited them much after Mila's fall, and when Jordan had turned up at the vineyard Greg hadn't got involved. Not that Jordan had given him a chance to. Jordan hadn't spoken about it—not the accident, not his wife. The only reason he had been there was because Mila hadn't wanted him around. That was the first time he had noticed the anger seep in, the resentment. The signs that he had it in him to react as his father had after his mother's death.

Jordan reached for his glass of wine at the unsettling thought.

'But then you left.' She looked up at him. 'I'd like to say your father and I helped each other through it, but that isn't true. Like with everyone else...I pushed him away. I wanted nothing to do with him since he only reminded me of you, and of what I'd lost.'

She cleared her throat, as though the admission had taken her by surprise. And since it had surprised *him*, too, he didn't interrupt.

'I was staying at the beach house—I couldn't stay at our place alone, not after what had happened—and I told Greg because I didn't want him to worry. And then I got the divorce papers, and Greg was the only person who would understand...'

She stopped, and he heard her take a shaky breath. He didn't blame her—her story was peppered with anecdotes that he wasn't sure she would have shared with him if they hadn't agreed on having an honest conversation.

'I could see that you leaving had hurt him. I'm

not saying that to hurt *you*, Jordan,' she said immediately, and he wondered what it was in his face that had told her he needed reassurance. 'I'm telling you because you need to know to move on. He was hurt, but I think he understood. He didn't blame you.'

'I'm not sure that's true.'

'It is,' she said firmly.

'You didn't know him like I knew him, Mila. And he asked me not to go. Told me I would be destroying our relationship if I did.' He could feel his breathing hitch, and he emptied his wine glass.

'Maybe that's true,' she said when he'd set the wine glass down, and he saw that she was watching him. 'But you didn't know him like *I* did either.'

He wondered what she meant by that—was about to ask—and then she continued, 'He was growing frailer, I saw. At first I thought it was because of everything that had happened over the last months. I'd lost some weight, too, so I didn't think too much of it. And then he had the first heart attack. He was out in the fields with Frank. They had people around them, who rallied round to get Greg to the car, to the hospital, the moment they realised what was happening. He wasn't alone.'

Jordan didn't know if she'd done it purposely, but that piece of information seemed to have settled something inside him.

'I didn't think twice when he asked me to move in after that. It was the only admission of needing help that he would ever give, I knew. So I moved in…helped around the house.'

'How long?'

She took a moment to respond, and then she said, 'The time between his first and second heart attacks was short, and between his second and third even shorter.' She was watching him carefully. 'The whole period was just over seven months.'

Seven months. It was shorter than the time his mother had had to suffer, and that comforted him. They'd found out about her cancer when Jordan was two, and she'd had to suffer for three long, agonising years—two without treatment and one with—before she'd passed away.

He thought of watching his mother suffer, and of how his father had suffered because of the pain he'd seen his wife go through. Felt relief that he hadn't been there to witness what Greg had gone through during the past year, and the overwhelming guilt at the thought. And realised how exactly his childhood had impacted him...

'Was he in pain? My father?'

The words escaped his lips before he'd realised he wanted to know the answer. But knowing the answer would confirm what he had just learned about himself—that he couldn't see anyone he cared about suffer.

The compassion in her eyes sent a blow to his heart. 'Sometimes. It made him miserable, difficult. More so than usual.' She paused. 'But it also made him more honest than usual.'

He raised his eyebrows, but she shook her head. 'I'm not going to tell you about that until you share something with me.'

The calm tone of her voice infuriated him. 'Tit for tat? Are we children?'

'If that's what it takes.' She shrugged, but the gesture was anything but casual.

'You have no right to keep things from me!' he spat, his heart pounding furiously. 'He was my father.'

'And maybe I wouldn't have to keep things from you if you'd been here.'

'Back to this, are we?' He shook his head and thought that he needed to get out of the room.

'Yes, we are. But we wouldn't need to get back to it if you just *told* me why you left,' she shot back.

'Because of *you*,' he said angrily. 'You wouldn't listen to me, just like my mother didn't listen to my father. And where did *that* get her?'

He was breathing heavily, and it took him a moment to compose himself.

'What does that mean?' she asked in a shaky voice when he finally looked at her.

Her face had lost its colour, and it shook him more than he wanted it to. 'It doesn't matter.'

'Yes, it does,' she said, in a voice that twisted his insides. 'Please, Jordan, just let me in for once.'

'You know more about me than anyone else.'

'I don't know *enough*,' she contradicted him. 'There's more—I know there's more. I've shared so much with you,' she said, in a tone that told him that that wasn't necessarily what she had wanted. 'Please, Jordan. I…I…*need* you to tell me.'

'I can't give you more than this, Mila,' he rasped, and pushed up from his seat. He didn't need to see the torment on her face when he had his own to deal with.

He walked out of the room, ignoring the voice that mocked him for running away from her for the second time.

CHAPTER FOURTEEN

MILA WATCHED HIM leave and pain tore through her. She had been honest with him. She had pushed through her reservations about opening up to him and told him she *needed* him.

And he'd rejected her.

She gasped when the pain turned into a burn that consumed her entire body, and sank to her knees. *This* was why she didn't want him back. *This* was exactly what she was afraid of. Showing people the real her, showing *him* the real her, and having them—*him*—reject her.

Though she didn't know how it was possible, this was worse than the first time. Maybe it was because then Jordan hadn't been leaving *her*. Not the real her. No, back then he'd been leaving the person she was pretending to be. The one who didn't believe that she was worth him, who didn't speak her mind, who was waiting—expecting—

for him to leave. The one who had failed as a mother, as a wife.

But since he'd come back she had shown him more and more of herself. She hadn't realised how much until right at that moment when she hadn't been able to hide behind the person she showed the world.

A sob escaped, but she clasped a hand over her mouth. She *wouldn't* let him hear her cry for him. She would get through this—she would. She had survived growing up without anyone to care for her.

It didn't matter now that the man she loved didn't care for her enough to be honest with her.

Another sob came when she realised the truth that she'd been running away from since Jordan had come back. She still loved him. She'd never stopped. That was why she had started opening up to him. Why she had told him the truth. Why she had shown him who she was. Maybe even why she wanted the event to go well—so she could show him, prove to him, that she was capable, that she was worthy.

She wanted Jordan to love the real her.

It was a foolish hope, she thought now. Not

because she wasn't worthy—she was slowly but surely fighting her way out of *that* pit—but because he didn't want to. She knew he was struggling—she had watched him during their conversation, knew that the information she'd given him about his father had opened up something for him—and now she knew that it had to do with his parents. With his mother. But, whatever it was, he didn't want *her* to be a part of it.

He doesn't need me, she thought, and closed her eyes against the pain.

She'd always thought it was something simple—something childish, even—to feel needed. To want a family who would need her unconditionally. But it wasn't, and she needed to face that. She needed to stop *pretending* that she was okay without having it, and to *really* be okay with it.

The man she loved didn't need her. She wouldn't ever get to have the family she had always wanted. And that was okay, she told herself. She would get through it. She *would* be okay.

But that didn't have to happen right now, she thought as she lowered her head between her knees and let the tears fall silently to the floor.

* * *

Jordan got up earlier than he normally would the next day. Not only because he hadn't got any sleep, but because he knew Mila was an early riser and he wanted to be up before her. He wasn't running away, he told himself. He just needed to get out of the house to think.

He sighed when he heard a loud thunderclap, and then the steady pelting of rain on the roof. There would be no walking through the vineyard to clear his thoughts, he thought. But since he was already up he decided to get some coffee. He needed the strength.

He had hurt her. The look on her face when she'd told him she needed him to let her in would be branded in his mind for ever. He wished that he could go back, that he could take it back, so that they could go back to the truce they'd had with one another. But he couldn't, and now all he wanted was to finish the darn event and get it over with so that he could move on with his life.

Because he didn't want to get caught up in the past any more. The last few days had been more than enough for his entire lifetime, and he could do without the memories of his mother, without the regrets he had about his father.

And he could do without Mila.

His hand stilled midway on its path to bringing the coffee mug to his mouth. That *was* what he was saying, wasn't it? She was the one forcing him to face his past. The last few days had been filled with his past because of *her*. And since he wanted the event over and done with, it meant he wanted things with *her* to be over and done with...right?

Except that the very thought sent an unpleasant frisson through his body. And an even worse one through his heart. The last thing he wanted was to say goodbye to her. Though they'd been difficult for him, the past few days had also been great. He'd started to get to know a side of Mila that he hadn't seen before. In fact, he'd thought he was getting to know a whole different Mila. The feistiness, the speaking her mind suited her in a way he hadn't considered before.

But it was more than that. It was the passion that he could see she had for her job. For her family. Because, although she didn't think she had one, the way she cared about Lulu and his father was more familial than anything he had ever experienced.

She was compassionate even when she didn't want to be, he thought as he remembered the way she had cared for him after his run-in with Lulu. As he thought about how she'd had nothing to gain when his father had asked her to move in with him and yet she had still done it.

It spoke of warmth, of the kindness that was naturally *her*. She was the best person he knew. And he cared about her.

But he couldn't *be* with her.

Not when she needed more from him than he could give her. So he would simply have to be without her. And even though the thought sent pain through him, he knew it was the right thing.

But that didn't mean he didn't have to apologise to her. He'd been a bit of a jerk the previous day, walking out on her like that, and she didn't deserve it. Not when *he* had been the person to suggest they have an honest conversation in the first place.

He started taking out things for breakfast. It was an apology, yes, but he also wanted to see her smile again. He wanted to see the smile that made him feel as if he was the only person in the world. The smile that pierced through his defences and reminded him of why he had fallen in love with her...

Before he could ponder why seeing her smile had become so important, she walked in. She stopped when she saw him there, and he could sense her hesitation. And then she turned around.

'Hey, I'm making breakfast.'

She stopped, and then slowly turned back to him. 'Are we just going to pretend last night didn't happen?'

Her voice was a little husky, her hair still mussed from sleep, and the effect was potent. It was as if his body was reminding him about yet another thing he was leaving behind, and it took a moment for him to recover.

'I'm trying to apologise.'

'Why? What's the point?'

His heart dribbled against his chest when he realised he didn't have an answer for her.

'Because we have an event to plan together,' he finally managed.

'If that's the only reason, apology not accepted.

I've worked with people I don't like before. This won't be a first for me.'

She turned away from him again, and his heart skidded to a halt when he realised that she was putting barriers up. Barriers he didn't think would ever come down again. It bothered him and he didn't know why.

'We're doing more than just working together, Mila,' he found himself saying.

'Really?' She folded her arms. 'What else are we doing, then?'

'We're saying goodbye to my father.' That wasn't it, he realised as his stomach sank. But it was good enough to appease her.

'You know where to hit, don't you?' she said as her arms dropped to her sides.

She was right, but he couldn't think of anything else to say. Not when he was still stunned by how all his conclusions earlier had been swept aside the minute he'd seen her. How much the thought that she would push him away again had alarmed him. How much he wanted things between them to be okay.

'How about we start with a cup of coffee?' she

said when he didn't respond, and he nodded, turning away from her.

Why was it suddenly so important for him to stay close to her? He had resigned himself to letting go—of her, of the past—but now he couldn't imagine anything worse.

He took his time making her coffee, ignoring the sudden jittery feeling in his body, and then he handed it to her carefully, so that they wouldn't touch. But her fingers brushed against his anyway, and his body responded.

Except that the physical effect she had on him had little to do with desire. It was a way of confirming what he had just realised. He still had feelings for her. It was the only thing that made his reaction to her logical. What else could make his rational thoughts seem like the most nonsensical things in the world?

He had barely acknowledged his feelings before he was striding towards her. He took the mug from her hands, had the pleasure of seeing her eyes widen and hearing her sharp inhalation, and then with her body against his, he touched his lips to hers.

She tasted of coffee and toothpaste…a combination he would have never thought sexy if he hadn't experienced it himself. She didn't move at first, her lips stiff under his, and he prepared himself to pull back—all but had words of apology ready in his mind before he felt her hands tentatively touch his waist.

Immediately he felt heat at their contact, but he resisted giving in to it. Instead he kept it slow, like the afternoon walks they'd used to take on Sundays, and let the fire simmer. It made him more aware of the connection they shared, of how their kiss was more than just a meeting of their lips, more than just something he was doing to sate his need for her.

It made slow and tender feel as satisfying and as passionate as the desperate kiss they had shared—was it only the previous day?

He didn't spend much time thinking about it—was too consumed by the way her body fitted his in just the right way. By the way her hands tightened on his waist, and then slid up under his shirt to touch his skin. Everywhere they moved heightened the sensation in his body, and he sank deeper into the kiss, using his tongue to remind her of their passion, of their love.

She moaned, pressed herself tighter against him, and he felt her shake. It turned the temperature up between them and his hands found her waist and lifted her up, setting her on the kitchen counter without losing contact. She pulled the hoodie he wore over his head, and he barely felt the sting of cold on his bare body. Not when she was kissing his neck, his shoulders, then his mouth again, as if she had discovered she needed him just as much as he needed her.

The thought gave him pause, and he moved away.

'Do you want this?' he asked, and searched her face for the real answer.

His heart was filled by her beauty in that moment—the flush of her cheeks, her untamed curls framing her face, her chest heaving—but he couldn't ignore the flash of uncertainty, of fear that lit her face.

It was gone in a moment and she nodded and pulled his head closer, but with all the self-control inside him, he resisted.

'You don't, Mila. At least, you're not sure,' he forced himself to say, and braced himself against the pain that flashed through her eyes at his words.

'No, I think *you're* the one who isn't sure,' she told him.

'You have no idea what I'm thinking,' he said, his voice sharp. She was too close to the truth.

'Whose fault is that?' she asked softly, before pushing at his chest.

He took a step back, watched as she lowered herself off the counter and pulled at the shirt that had ridden up to her waist during their passion. But not before he had got a good look at her stomach. The skin was slightly loose over the flat surface, with tiny vertical lines leading to the scar from her C-section—evidence that she had once carried his child—and his hands itched to touch, to feel, to remind himself of better times between them.

'I don't know what to do about you,' she said suddenly, and all his thoughts gave way to one single thought that ripped at his heart.

He was hurting her.

With his words, with his actions. He couldn't do this with her again, he realised. Not until he was sure.

'I'm sorry,' he said, because he didn't know what else he could say.

'We should just stick to the event, Jordan. Everything else...'

She looked at him, her eyes shockingly beautiful in their misery, and he saw for the first time that they were a little swollen, a little red, as if she'd been crying. The thought sent another blow to his heart.

'*Nothing* else will work between us.'

She walked away, leaving him alone in the kitchen. It was sobering to think that he had never felt so alone ever before. He no longer had his mother, his father. He no longer had his wife.

He was pushing her away.

Was it worth it? Was his guilt, his regret over what had had happened in his childhood, over his relationship with his father, over his mother's choices, worth risking the woman he loved?

He ran a hand through his hair and then slid it down his face. Who was he fooling? Thinking he had feelings for Mila was just vague enough to make him feel better about himself. But he should have known the truth would catch up with him. He should have known from the moment he had seen her and fallen for her that he couldn't run away from his feelings for her.

His shoulders stiffened even more at the thought. He needed to stop running. He loved Mila—had never stopped—and he needed to step up for her. Except...he didn't know how. Or even if he could. He had been running away all his life. From the moment his father had told him that his mother had chosen to look after him instead of her own health. From the moment he'd realised his father blamed Jordan for her death.

Even the thought sent waves of hurt through him, and only his hope of love with Mila was keeping them at bay. He knew that if he told her those hurts might overwhelm him, and that if he didn't they would keep nudging at him, causing him to run all his life.

He had to make a choice. And, despite all the things he had been through in his life, despite all the difficult choices he'd had to make, he knew that this one would be the worst.

CHAPTER FIFTEEN

SHE KEPT MAKING the same mistakes, and if she continued down that path it would destroy her. So Mila kept to her word and focused on her work, ignoring the kiss that she'd shared with Jordan that morning—*and* its after-effects.

She called Lulu and explained that their event was now less than two weeks away and they needed to make sure there *would* be an event. She confirmed the details with Simon, informed the marquee supplier about the date, and called to tell the vendors the same thing. She soothed complaints, found alternatives, until eventually she was fairly certain that the event would take place.

She updated Mark, as the executor of the will, and emailed him records of all they had done to keep within the conditions of the will.

And then she braced herself for visiting her house again.

She had decided the previous evening that she would move out of Greg's house. She should have done it the day after Jordan had returned. It would have saved her so much heartache. Now her heart pained her with every beat, and her mind was consumed by grief because he didn't want her.

He wanted her physically, maybe, she thought, flushing at the memory of that morning, but not in any other way. And so, because she couldn't live with the man who reminded her of everything she wanted and couldn't have, she was going to live at the house where they'd started their lives together.

It was better that way, she told herself as she began packing a bag. She would start clearing the house, get it on the market, and once it was sold she would use the money to buy offices for her business.

She and Lulu had used to work out of the flat she'd rented before she got married and at Lulu's home before Mila's fall, but now she wanted something more legitimate. Something that would make her feel steady. Something that was her own.

It was also the only thing she could think of to use the money from the sale of the house *for*—taking it to live a lavish life didn't seem right to her. And she knew Jordan wouldn't want it back—it would be a slap in the face to him if she offered, when she knew that he'd done it because he had wanted to give her something. He had hurt her, yes, but Mila had no intention of doing the same thing to him. She was better than that.

That was another reason why she had decided to sort out the house on her own. Before she'd thought she needed him. That she couldn't do it by herself. But as part of her resolution to move on, to only rely on herself, she *would* do it by herself.

Yes, her heart still thumped at the thought of going back to the house where she had lost her baby, but it was also the house where she had found out she was going to have him. It was the place where she had first felt him kick, where she had spent the only time she'd had with him. And although focusing on those positives almost made her reconsider selling—*almost*—she knew it would be for the best if she did.

And then, when the event was over, she would file for divorce.

She *would* move on from Jordan.

She packed the case with her essentials—she had enough clothing to last her until the event at the house—and dragged the case behind her to the front door. It rattled on the tiles, and then stopped. She turned back, giving it a forceful pull before continuing.

And walked straight into Jordan.

'Hey!' he said, steadying her, and she had a flashback to those hands on her waist, lifting her. 'Where are you going?'

'I'm going to stay somewhere else.' She knew it sounded snappy, but it was better than showing the need that heated her belly at her memories.

She looked up at him and saw the carefully blank look in his eyes.

'You're leaving,' he said flatly.

'I am,' she said in the same tone. 'It's what's best, isn't it?'

She could almost see the gears grinding in his head as he thought, and she wondered what there was to think about. He'd made his choice. She'd made hers. That was it.

That was it, she reminded herself when something inside her lit up—just a little—at the thought of him wanting her to stay.

'Where are you going?'

'Back to the house.'

She saw the twitch in his eyebrow before he schooled his features again. 'I'll take you.'

'No, no,' she said quickly, feeling all her bravado fade at the prospect of going back with him. 'I'm calling a taxi.'

'No, you're not.'

She would have been annoyed by his tone if she hadn't seen that twitch in his brow again. She had grown familiar with his facial expressions when they were married—was even more so now, perhaps—and she knew he was upset, but was trying to hide it.

'Please, just let me do this thing for you.'

The tone had softened, and she hated that her heart did the same. 'Okay…'

She didn't protest when he took the case from her hand, and she followed him to the car, getting in before he could open the door for her. She had had too many lingering touches from him in the past when he'd done that, and she wasn't interested in repeating it now. Not when she was already warning her heart to stay behind the wall she'd erected the previous night after she had finished sobbing. That wall had already been threatened by their kiss that morning, and she refused to put it in danger again.

When they pulled into the driveway at the house she immediately turned to get out—and then froze when she felt his hand on her thigh. It was in no way sexual, but heat seeped through her and she turned back in the hope that if she did he would remove it.

'Are you going to miss it?' he asked, and pulled back his hand as Mila had hoped.

He was staring at the house now, avoiding her gaze, so she sat back and looked at it, too. It *was* beautiful, she thought, and felt a pang in her heart.

'I am,' she said carefully.

'But it's not the vineyard?' he replied and looked at her.

She felt pinned by the look—especially since he had said exactly what she was thinking. The house she had lived in for the past year had begun to feel like more of a home to her than this place, where she had lived in with the man she had married. It was going to be hard to leave all that behind, she thought.

'I walked in here for the first time and I thought this would be a great house for you to come home to. Your first real home. I wanted it to be special for you.'

And just like that his words carved another spot in her heart.

'It *was* special,' she said, 'and it will always be my first home. Thank you.'

She wanted to kiss him in gratitude—a simple peck as she would have given him so often before—but she resisted.

'I'd like to show you something.'

He got out of the car before she could answer and she followed quickly, unsure of what was going on.

'I wanted to show it to you yesterday, but we... er...got a little distracted.'

He locked the car, and then held out his hand to her. It was a simple gesture, almost a reflex, but he stood like that until she walked over to him and carefully took his hand with her own. The warmth immediately gave her comfort, and she almost pulled away. She didn't need to be reminded of how much Jordan made her feel at home. But then she looked up, saw the impact simply taking her hand had had on him, and left it there.

You're hopeless, she berated herself.

But still she followed—perhaps because she thought it was for the last time.

'Where are you taking me?' she asked, to escape her thoughts.

'You'll see,' he replied, and she felt him tighten his grip on her hand.

It made her sad, and she wasn't completely sure why. They walked in silence, and when they reached a gate that Mila had never seen before Jordan took a key out of his pocket.

'Wait—this is the Gerber place.' Mila let go of his hand and placed hers lightly on his arm.

'It used to be,' he answered, and then pushed open the gate.

It didn't make any sound as it opened—confirmation to her that it had been recently put there—and Jordan gestured for her to go through. The plot was vast and green, as though completely unaffected by the coldness of the season, and a bridge led over the stream that ran around the whole property.

He held out a hand to help her cross, even though she saw that the bridge was fairly sturdy. And she took his hand, needing the contact to help her soothe the sudden anxiety in her stomach.

'I don't think this is a good idea.'

'Trust me.'

She stood at the base of the bridge, looked at the sincerity in his eyes, and felt the wall she had prided herself on erecting and then maintaining completely disintegrate. She nodded, unable to speak, and they walked over the wooden bridge together.

She ran her free hand over the railing, forcing herself to focus on its design—anything to keep her mind occupied with something other than how much she loved him. It was a perfect example of the traditional charm that all the Stellenbosch properties had—just as the barn they were walking towards now was.

'Are you going to tell me what's going on?' Mila asked softly.

'This is the latest Thomas property.'

'You *own* this place?'

'Yeah.'

'How? It must be recent, because I didn't once see or suspect that the Gerbers were selling their property.'

'They weren't planning on selling it, but I managed to convince them.'

He stuffed his hands into his pockets, and the gesture made him seem less rich-vineyard-owner and more handsome-husband. Though his words implied that he had very much *played* rich vineyard owner to get the property.

'When?'

'About a year ago.'

'A year ago? But that was—'

'Just before your fall?'

She nodded, and he continued.

'Yes, it was. I was going to surprise you with it after you gave birth.'

'With what? Another property? We didn't need that—'

'With the Thomas Events venue.'

Her mind took a moment to process what he was saying, and the moment she did she felt the heat of tears in her eyes.

'The Thomas Events venue?' she repeated, and hated it that it sounded so right. Hated it even more that Jordan had been trying to make another dream of hers come true.

She wished with all her might that things could have worked out between them. Her life would have been absolutely perfect then! She would have had a place to go home to, a husband who loved her and a baby who needed her and to whom she would have given the world.

'I thought it was time your business had a home,' Jordan said when she didn't say anything. 'I had the barn redone so that you could host events there—weddings, conferences, anything you wanted—and I was going to turn the house into an office. You could meet your clients there, do mock-ups—even turn one of the rooms into a baby's room, if you wanted.'

'I...um... Wow... I...' She took a deep breath, and pulled her hand away from his. 'This is... I don't know what to say, Jordan.'

A tear slid down her face and he took a step forward.

'I didn't want you to be sad. I just wanted to—'

'What?' she asked, grasping for anger instead

of pain. 'You wanted to show me another thing I don't have?'

'*No!* No, of course not,' he said quickly, his eyes wide. 'I wanted to show you this because it's still yours. I want you to have it.'

'I don't *want* it,' she snapped, and another tear rolled down her face. 'I don't want any reminder of the life we will never have together.'

'Mila—' He stepped forward again, opening his arms, but she took a step back away from him.

'No, Jordan! You don't get it, do you? I can't do this with you any more. I can't pretend that we're friends, or whatever we're pretending to be at the moment.' She took a shaky breath and impatiently wiped at her tears. 'I need to move on. I *am* moving on. The minute this event is over, I'm gone. Far away from this place—' she threw a hand out '—from the house I lived in as your wife and from the vineyard that started this whole thing in the first place.'

She looked up at him and choked out her next words.

'I'm filing for divorce and moving on from *you*.'

She bit her lip, trying to compose herself as the words tore her heart into pieces.

And then she said slowly, 'I don't want you to show me things I'll never get to enjoy. And I don't want you to show me a person I'll never get to be with.'

'No, Mila—wait,' he said when she turned to walk away, and she heard anger and something else coating his voice with gravel. 'You had your say, so now I'm having mine. I showed you this because it's *yours*. I don't care what you call it, or if you accept it or not. I bought this for *you*. So that you can understand how much I care for you and how much I believe in you.'

Care, she thought. Present tense. Before she could caution herself against it, she felt hope re-ignite.

'You can move on, move away, Mila, but this place will still be here when you get back.' There was a momentary pause, and then he said, 'It'll be waiting for you just like I will be.'

He took a step closer and lifted her chin until she was looking at him.

'I don't care whether it's a year or ten years,

whether we're married or not, I'll be waiting for you.'

'Why?' she whispered, before her mind could give her permission to speak.

There was barely a moment before he answered, 'Because I love you.'

He slid an arm around her waist and pulled her in, silencing her protests even before his mouth found hers. It was similar to the way she had kissed *him* two days ago, she thought hazily, and she wondered if his reason was similar, too—to show her that they mattered.

But she was already too lost in the taste of him to think any more about it. Her body was thanking her for something—*someone*—it had longed for but never got in the last year. And yet still she could feel a part of her resist—the sane, rational part of her that wanted to protect her poor already broken heart—and in response she felt his arm loosen around her.

He was giving her an out—telling her that she could leave the embrace if she wanted to.

But that only made her want him more, and barely a beat after he'd offered her a way out, she found herself pressed against him again. His arms went around her, tighter this time, and his mouth took hers more deeply, hungry after the possibility of stopping.

She couldn't breathe, couldn't hear, couldn't think in his arms, and she poured all the love she felt for him into the kiss, turning it from desperate into tender.

He eased away, and then looked down at her, his eyes heavy with need. 'I love you, Mila.'

Hearing the words again was like a slap. 'Stop!' She pulled herself away from him completely and felt the tears come back. 'You don't mean that.'

'Of *course* I mean it,' he said firmly, almost angrily. But the look in his eyes was...*fear*.

'If you really meant that, Jordan, you would stop being afraid of sharing with me and tell me about your childhood. About your mother and your father. You would *want* to tell me about it.'

CHAPTER SIXTEEN

JORDAN OPENED HIS MOUTH, ready to retort, but she had hit him exactly where she knew he was most vulnerable. He closed his mouth again, and before he could think of something to respond with she spoke again.

'This is exactly what I'm talking about. *Why* is it so hard for you to tell me about it?'

'For the same reasons you don't talk to me about *your* childhood in foster care.'

Her head snapped back as though he had hit her, and something inside him warned him to stop. But the words kept sprinting out of his mouth.

'It isn't that easy to talk about when you're on the other side, is it?' he said steadily, and watched the emotions run over her face like a movie reel.

Eventually she replied, 'No, it isn't. But when you love someone you have to make a sacrifice and put your reservations aside.' She took a deep breath. 'I didn't have anyone who needed me when I was growing up, Jordan. I lived with ten different families in eighteen years. It was hard.'

She blew out a shaky breath, and he felt himself shake a little, too. Was she doing what he thought she was?

'I didn't have anyone who needed me, and quite frankly no one wanted me. Lulu was the first person I met who cared about me—and I mean *really* cared—and I was sixteen years old when I met her.'

She wiped at tears he hadn't seen, too captivated by what she was telling him to notice before—and even more so by what it meant.

'Growing up like that made me... It made me someone I don't want to be any more.' She shrugged. 'I wouldn't ever say what I felt or what I thought because I wanted people to like me.'

'Even with me?' he asked, needing to know.

She looked at him through wet lashes that made her eyes all the more piercing. 'Even with you.' She bit her lip, and then said, 'I couldn't... I *thought* I couldn't tell you what I felt. There was a big part of me that felt like being married to you was a dream, and I didn't want to wake up. It didn't matter how I felt about our house, our cars...'

All things *he* had chosen for her, he thought in disgust.

'I had you. And that was enough for me.'

She lifted a hand when he opened his mouth to speak.

'Wait, I'm not done yet. I have to get this out before you say anything.'

Something shifted in her eyes, and panic spread through his body in response.

This is the last time she'll do this, he thought, and his heart pounded at the thought of losing her.

'But that also meant I didn't know how to ask you for help when we lost our child. I was afraid that you blamed me—you'd asked me to slow down and I hadn't. And then I fell down the stairs and I thought that you were right—I *should* have slowed down, enjoyed being pregnant. After that...I felt like a failure. Like every fear of mine had come true.'

Tears shone in her eyes and he took a step forward, wanting to be closer to her, to comfort her.

'It was a confirmation of what I'd feared all

along—that I wasn't worthy of you. I always expected you to leave me, so when you did—'

'I proved you right,' he finished for her, stunned.

How could he have been so unaware of what his wife was going through? How had he not noticed that she hadn't ever disagreed with him? How had he been so blind? She had it completely wrong, he thought. *He* was the one who wasn't worthy of *her*.

'Mila, I'm so sorry. I didn't know...'

He trailed off as he realised that she had just told him everything he had ever wanted to know about her. And based on that information—based on the completely raw look in her eyes—he knew how much it had cost her.

'You love me, too.'

He didn't need her to say it because it was suddenly so painfully clear to him. It made the fact that he felt as if he was losing her so much worse. He looked at her, saw the truth in her eyes, and the past year of his life flashed through his mind.

He had always been a loner, but he hadn't ever felt alone. As difficult as his relationship with his father had been, Jordan had always known he had somewhere to go to, someone to talk to if he needed it. But after he had left for Johannesburg he hadn't really spoken to his father. His life had felt emptier than he'd thought possible, and he'd felt more alone than ever.

He had missed Mila with all of him, and now he knew—he *knew*—that his grief at losing his son, at losing his chance of a full family, would have been bearable if he had been with Mila.

It was something her words had only just made him realise, and the simple truth of it led him to say, 'My father blamed me for my mother's death.'

When the words were out, he couldn't believe such a simple sentence could convey the thing that had followed him around for his entire life. He stuffed his hands in his pockets and faced the stream. He didn't want to see her face—the compassion he knew would be there—while he told her of his childhood. Not when what he was going to tell her might change her opinion of his father, whom she'd clearly cared about.

He rubbed a hand over his face, wondering where to start, and decided on the part Mila already knew about.

'My mom found out about her cancer when I was two.' He took a steadying breath, then continued, 'She refused treatment. For two years she didn't want to get treatment, even though she was ill most of the time... She wanted to be a normal mother.'

He took another breath, shifted the weight between his feet.

'Her mom had died of the same thing, and they'd caught it earlier. She'd had treatment and it hadn't helped. So she refused. She thought the treatment would only make her sicker, even if only for a little while, and she didn't want to lose any time with me. So she chose to be a mother. She chose *me*.'

Jordan shrugged, the movement heavy with the weight he had been carrying. With the guilt.

'My dad hated her choice. He told me once that he'd begged her every day for those two years to get treatment, until finally he wore her down. And during that time my dad kept me at a distance. He wouldn't sit with her when she watched me play—would only agree to family time if she was there.'

Jordan wondered how his memories of the

events he was talking about could be vague, but the feelings they evoked still sharp.

'He helped to take care of me physically—especially when my mom grew weaker, more ill—but he wouldn't be a father to me. Not a real one. But he was the *best* husband, and even at my age I knew that he loved her more than anything. By the time she agreed to treatment it was too late.'

He felt her move closer to him, and welcomed the comfort her presence brought.

'She spent her last year in agony, going through a cycle of chemo and radiation, until finally my dad brought her home and she died in her sleep a few days later.'

'It wasn't your fault,' she said, in a voice thick with emotion.

'I didn't think so until...'

This was probably one of the worst parts, he thought, but he pushed through.

'For years after my mom died, I felt like I was walking on eggshells. My father was testy most of the time, and I just got used to trying to make myself invisible at home. But at school, I acted out. And one day...' He took a deep breath. 'One day I did something I can't even remember any more and my dad got called in to school. I remember he sat there, listening to my teacher, and I saw the tic just above his eye. I didn't know what that meant then, but when I got home...'

He paused, then forced himself to say the words.

'The anger that my dad had built up since my mom had died came spilling out of his mouth.' Jordan's jaw clenched. 'He told me that if it hadn't been for me my mom wouldn't have died. He said that it was *my* fault, that she had foregone treatment because of me, and that it had all been for nothing since I was just a bratty, ungrateful child.'

Jordan stopped for a moment, composing himself.

'He said some other things that night—I think most of them things he blamed himself for. He broke down immediately afterwards and apologised, over and over again. It was grief, mixed with anger and regret, but I've never forgotten how seeing my distant father break down felt. Or...' he turned to her now '...how it affected me.'

He could see the sadness gleaming in her eyes,

and he waited for resentment to boil up in him at the sight of it. But it never came, and he realised that the only thing he felt was her support.

'I always wondered why things were so difficult between you two,' she said after a while, and she walked over until she was next to him and took his hand.

The warmth of her gesture of comfort immediately flowed through him, and he tightened his grip. 'I didn't think you'd noticed.'

She let out a slight laugh. 'It was hard not to. I always thought it was because of him.'

'Why?'

'He was a difficult man, Jordan. He didn't show his emotions, didn't say what he thought, and most of the time when he spoke it sounded like a military command.'

Floored, he looked down at her. 'I thought you *liked* him?'

'I loved him,' she corrected. 'He was kind to me, and in his own way he showed me he cared for me. I *loved* him,' she repeated, and he could hear the grief in her voice, 'but that doesn't mean I didn't see his flaws.'

He nodded, and there was a silence as they both

thought about his father. As he thought about the fact that he needed to continue with his story.

'He only became the man you're talking about after that night. But even then he wasn't perfect, and I spent my whole life believing that my mother's death was my fault.'

'Your father was angry, Jordan. He was grieving for a woman he had loved with all of him and for the life he thought he would get to live. He didn't mean what he said, *or* the things he did.'

'But she *did* choose me, Mila,' he said softly.

'Exactly. *She* did. You had absolutely no say over the choices she made, Jordan. Don't keep blaming yourself for something you didn't have any control over.' She wrapped an arm around him. 'It won't help.'

Somewhere in his mind her words resonated, and he said, 'I didn't want to see you suffer like she did.'

She looked up at him, her eyes wide. '*That's* why you left?'

'I didn't think so at first. I thought I was doing the right thing.' He stopped, wondering how he was having all the most difficult conversations of his life within the space of an hour. 'But I've realised over the last few days that that *was* why I left. Why I ran.'

Her arm was still around him, though he could feel it slacken.

You deserve it for being a coward, he thought, but it didn't make the pain of her pulling away any easier.

Still he continued. If she was going to leave—if she was going to move on—it wouldn't be because he hadn't fought for her with all his might.

'It was also because I was...*angry.* I couldn't deal with the loss of our son.'

It was his biggest regret about his father's death—that he hadn't been able to tell Greg that he understood the grieving. He had been too young with his mother, but losing his son... Finally Jordan had understood how irrational grief could be.

'I got angry at you for pushing me away, and it...it scared me. I thought I was turning into my father. Even after the anger had dulled I thought it was for the best that I didn't come back, that I didn't fight for us. Because I didn't want to wake up one day and blame you for something that wasn't your fault. I didn't want to treat you like my father had treated me.'

He paused.

'It wasn't your fault, Mila,' he said again, because he thought she needed to know. 'The fall had nothing to do with you not slowing down. You would have had plenty of time to do that later. We *both* would have.' He turned to her. 'You need to let go of whatever's still inside you that thinks the accident was your fault.'

With eyes full of tears, she nodded, and his heart settled at the knowledge of what they'd just shared. He had finally told her everything, and he hoped he had got her to forgive herself. If she chose to leave now, she would leave free of the weight of the past. But still he wished she wouldn't leave, and his heart sank when she pulled away, convinced that she had given up on him.

So much so that he looked up in surprise when he saw she was in front of him.

She took both of his hands in hers. 'I wish you'd told me about this a long time ago.'

'I couldn't.'

'And I wouldn't have been in the right space to

listen,' she agreed, and then took a deep breath. 'It makes sense now. All of it.'

'But does it change anything?' he asked hopefully, and a familiar expression shone in her eyes. One he hadn't seen in almost a year.

'I...I think that depends on you.'

The glimmer of affection in her eyes that he'd seen just before gave way to seriousness.

'Are you still angry at me?'

'No, not any more. I understand why you pushed me away. I understand *you* better, too.'

She gave him a small smile. 'Do you still blame yourself for your mom?'

'I...' He took a breath. 'I think it'll take some time—just like I think it will for you not to blame yourself for the baby—but we'll get there.'

She nodded, gripping his hands tightly. 'You won't turn into your father, Jordan, so I won't even ask if you still believe you will.'

'How do you *know*?'

'Because I know *you*. You're strong, and when you're not afraid...' she squeezed his hand '...you're the most considerate man I know.' She paused, and then dropped his hands to slide her arms around his waist. 'And because you have me, and I will make sure that you don't turn into an angry, bitter person. Our little grape wouldn't have wanted that for his father.'

His heart filled at her words. 'You're staying with me?'

'If you want me, I'd really like to.'

'I don't want you, Mila. I *need* you.' He pulled her in tighter and felt the part of him that had been broken heal. 'I love you so much.'

'I love *you*,' she replied, and when she pulled back her eyes were gleaming with tears.

'Don't cry,' he said gently, wiping her cheeks.

'They're happy tears,' she whispered. 'I didn't dare imagine this was possible when you came back, but my heart hoped it would be.'

'Mine, too,' he said, knowing that his heart was only full when he was with her.

'And we'll face everything we go through now together.'

'I promise.' He stopped, and then said gently, 'I want us to have another baby.'

He watched her, saw the fear.

'Not right now. When we're ready—when we've taken the time to *be* ready. You're going to be a wonderful mother, and I want a chance to be a good father. And a good husband to my pregnant wife.'

He smiled, lifted her chin. Noted that the fear had turned into longing.

'We can be a *family*, Mila.'

Another tear slipped down her face. 'It sounds perfect.' And then she smiled. 'How about we seal this with a kiss?'

He laughed and leaned down to kiss her, vowing that he wouldn't spoil his second chance at love with the woman who had always owned his heart.

CHAPTER SEVENTEEN

MILA FELT JORDAN'S hand tighten on hers and she sent him a grateful smile. It was the morning of their event—just over a week since their reconciliation—and she'd told Jordan that she wanted to visit their son's grave. She'd only ever been to the grave twice—when they'd buried him, and when they'd buried Greg. But after spending the past week talking with Jordan, sharing things that they hadn't shared with anyone else before, rebuilding their trust and fortifying the foundations of their new relationship, she finally found herself ready.

It didn't seem right to go through the event without doing it first, so they'd driven over and were now standing just in front of the path that would take them to the grave.

Except now, of course, her legs felt like lead and she didn't think she could do it.

'We can do this,' Jordan said, and she looked over, wondering if she had spoken out loud.

He threaded his fingers through hers and squeezed again, and she returned the pressure, knowing that he was just as nervous as she was. Probably even more so, since it was the first time he'd been back after his father's funeral, too.

Together they walked down the path that led to the family plot Greg had bought after his wife had died. He'd wanted to make sure that the Thomas family would always be together, even in death.

She slid an arm around Jordan's waist when they stopped in front of the first tombstone—made of the most expensive marble—which told her that Jade Thomas, Jordan's mother, had only lived until she was forty.

Way too young, she thought, thinking about how much time with her Greg had been robbed of...how early Jordan had lost her. She knew from losing her own parents how growing up without them could hurt. Perhaps it hurt even more, she considered, when you actually knew them.

'She would have been proud of you,' she said, leaning her head against Jordan's shoulder.

He lifted his arm and pulled her in closer. 'Even though I didn't look after my dad like she asked?' he said, but it was half-hearted, and she knew it reflected habit more than what he believed now.

'I think she would understand,' Mila replied softly, knowing that the tales she'd told Jordan about his mother—the ones Greg had shared with her in his rare open moments—confirmed her words. Jade had been a lovely woman: stubborn, like all the Thomases, but with just as big a heart as her son.

'I think she would, too,' Jordan said eventually, and they walked a few steps further to the front of Greg's grave. It was identical to Jordan's mother's, except that the words were about Greg.

'"Loving husband and father. You will be missed,"' she read aloud, and smiled. 'It's perfect, Jordan.' Her throat closed, but she smiled up at him. 'He *did* love you. Just in his own way.'

'I know.' Jordan laid a hand on the tomb and she waited, knowing that he needed time. 'I know that you loved me, Dad. I wish we could speak just one more time, so I could tell you I love you, too. So that I could tell you I understand now, and that I forgive you.' He took a shaky breath. 'But I think you already know that.'

Mila's heart broke for him, but she knew that it was healthy. It wouldn't do for him to keep it all in any more.

When he didn't say anything else, Mila said, 'Thank you for everything, Greg.' That was enough, she thought, but then she remembered something else. 'Especially for the will. Seems like your plan was right all along.'

They smiled at each other, and then took a few more moments to say goodbye. The overwhelming grief she had felt since Greg's death dulled to a throb in her heart, and that told her it would be okay. She and Jordan would be okay.

The tiny little tombstone that stood above the grave next to Greg's still broke her heart, though.

The name they'd decided on and had engraved that week was bold in grey against the black marble stone. Below the name was a black-and-white picture of her and Jordan on the day she had given birth—they both had tears on their faces, and were both clearly heartbroken, but she had her son in her arms and it was their only family photo.

The dates on his tombstone were the date they'd found out they were expecting their child and the date they'd lost him. And below that was an inscription.

You were the light of our lives.
A light that will stay in our hearts for ever.

'I still have that image of you in my head—you with our son in your arms...the absolute devastation and love on your face.' He sucked in air, and she felt the sucker punch of his emotions—*their* emotions—right down to her gut.

'Me, too. But with your face.'

She spoke because something inside her compelled her to. Perhaps because it was the first time they could acknowledge it together.

'The dreams I have are about that moment a lot. I had only just felt him alive inside me, and then when I could see him he wasn't.' She was whispering now, her voice no longer willing to say the words that told her the wound inside her was still fresh. 'I'm so glad you got to hold him while he was still alive.'

They clung to each other, and though she knew she was still healing she felt the glimmer of hope that sharing that moment with the only person who knew what she was going through had brought. Suddenly she was even more grateful for their second chance.

We'll do it right this time, baby, she told her son, and her lips curved even through the tears.

'He knows how much we love him.' Jordan's voice was raw as he spoke, but she saw the hope she felt inside reflected in his eyes.

'He does. I'm sure our parents tell him that every day.'

The thought of their family together made her smile widen.

'Yeah...' He looked down at her. 'I think so, too.'

It was a long time before either of them spoke again, but finally Jordan said, 'We should get going. Karen will probably be there for the soundcheck soon.'

They headed back to the car together, and before she climbed in Mila looked back one more time. 'We'll visit them again soon, won't we?'

Jordan kissed her hair. 'Of course.'

She smiled at him, and couldn't help but think

that the people they had visited would have loved it that she and Jordan were a family again.

'I'm sweating like a pig,' Lulu said, and fanned herself with the clipboard that she insisted on using for her tasks instead of the tablet Mila was using.

Mila laughed, grabbing a bottle of water from the ice bucket behind the stage that Karen had walked out onto a few minutes ago and handed it to her friend.

'The perks of growing a life inside you!'

Mila found she could say that now, after that morning, without a piercing pain going through her body. It was more like a dull ache in her heart that reminded her of her child, just like her significantly lowered fear of stairs. The necessity of this event had helped her overcome *that* fear, but she knew it was more than that, too. It was knowing that she *could* do it that helped her do it. And because of the person who had helped her reach that realisation.

'No!' Lulu said after gurgling down half the bottle. 'There is *no way* you can tell me that you're not getting as hot as I am.'

'Honey, it's eighteen degrees. We've spent the past half an hour handing out blankets to our guests and setting up the outside heaters. You *know* it's only you.'

'Maybe it's because I've been running around for the past week.'

'And you know I love you for it. Especially when you look at how amazingly it's turned out.'

She peeped out from the tent they had assembled backstage—just as they had for the first event—and a smile spread on her face.

The amphitheatre held about two hundred fifty people, which was about a hundred more than she had been expecting. Most of them were only there for Karen, but that didn't matter since they had all still bought food from the vendors, still purchased wine from the vineyard. They had managed to set up the marquee so that it had more than enough space for everyone, and as she looked up she was treated to a stunning view of the stars.

'It seems like a success.'

A voice broke through her thoughts and she turned to see Mark standing there, with a briefcase in one hand and some papers in the other, with Jordan behind him.

Her heart immediately responded to him being there, and she smiled at him before nervously asking Mark, 'Did we tick all the boxes?'

Mark pulled his glasses down from the top of his head and read from the paper in front of him. 'Well, your event *is* "under the stars"—excellent improvisation, by the way—and you have the same performer, you're screening the same movie, you have most of the vendors from the original event, and you've provided me with all the documentation for those who couldn't make it, as well as for their replacements. And you've done this all within the time limit.'

Mark removed his glasses.

'So I would say, yes. Congratulations, you two, you're officially the owners of Greg's share of the vineyard. I'll send the paperwork through in the coming weeks.'

Mark excused himself, and as soon as he was gone, Lulu let out a hoot.

'This is wonderful news, you guys!' She hugged them both, then waved a hand. 'But, much as I would like to celebrate with you, my bladder is telling me there are things that take a slightly higher priority at the moment.'

She winked at Jordan before she waddled off, and though that puzzled her Mila jumped into Jordan's arms the minute they were alone.

'We did it!' she said, her body sighing in contentment as soon as it touched his.

'We did.' He pulled back, and the look on his face made her heart thud.

'What's wrong?'

'There's just something... Actually, I can take care of it myself. I'll just run up to the house...'

He was already starting up the stairs by the time she'd processed his words, and in a bit of a panic she followed him.

'Jordan!' she called when they were far enough from the concert that they wouldn't be heard. 'Wait!'

She was out of breath when she finally caught up with him, and she rested her hands against her knees when she saw that he'd stopped.

'Why wouldn't you just wait for me?' she puffed, and then straightened. 'What's the problem—'

She broke off when she saw where they were, and a smile spread across her face.

'You are such a sneaky—'

He cut her off with a quick kiss, and then grinned as he pulled back.

'Surprise!' he said, and pushed open the gate to the place where they'd picnicked that very first night.

A blanket was spread out, just as it had been then, but this time there was a fire burning in the pit that had been created just in front of it. A bottle of Thomas Vineyard red wine was placed next to two glasses, and a variety of foods similar to those he'd had there the first time sat next to that.

'It's perfect,' she said with a smile as she turned towards him—and froze when she saw him kneeling in front of her.

'What are you *doing*?' she gasped. 'I've already told you I wouldn't file the papers.'

'I want to begin our second chance together properly, Mila.'

The teasing glint in his eyes was gone, replaced by a sincerity that sent a tear down her cheek.

'I can't live my life without you. I want you— and I need you—by my side for ever. I want to have a family with you, and I want to love you and our family unconditionally. Will you give me the chance to do that?'

She nodded, unable to speak, and he grinned.

'I'm not done yet.'

He pulled a ring from his pocket, and her heart skipped when she saw it was the one he'd proposed with the first time. The one she had put in a jewellery box the day she'd received the divorce papers and tried never to think about again.

'Be my wife again, Mila. And not only because we're still married.' He smiled. 'Marry me again.'

'Yes, of course—yes!' she said, and he slid the ring onto her finger.

She smiled at its familiar weight.

'I know the perfect time and the perfect place,' she said, and hooked her arms around his neck.

He grinned. 'Me, too. But until then...'

He kissed her, and she melted against him.

EPILOGUE

TWO DAYS LATER, on their second wedding anniversary, Mila stood in a long white dress covered in lace. Lulu beamed at her as she lowered the veil over Mila's face and dabbed at a tear that had fallen down her cheek.

'I'm such a mess!' Lulu said with a hiccup, and Mila smiled teasingly.

'The joys of—'

'Growing a life inside you—I know.' Lulu rolled her eyes and then smiled. 'I'm so happy for you.'

Mila laid a shaky hand on her stomach. 'Me, too.'

They walked the short distance from the house to the chapel where she and Jordan had made their vows two years before. And although she was wearing the same ring and the same dress as the first time they'd got married, *she* was a different person. She was someone who was more confident, who only cared about the opinions of those who loved her. And she was standing on her own this time.

Though she would have done anything to be walking down the aisle with Greg again, being on her own was oddly comforting. It represented the fact that she *could* be on her own if she needed to. But now she was walking towards the man who had promised her that she would never have to be alone again.

She didn't take her eyes off him as she walked down the short aisle, her heart thumping at how handsome he looked in his suit. And then it was just the two of them, standing in front of the altar, making their promises to one another.

'I can't believe how lucky I am to have you in my life again,' she began, and tears welled up in her eyes. 'You have shown me how it feels to be loved, to be needed. You have given me the family I've never had. You have helped me grow into someone I didn't know I could be. Into someone who is willing to hope after hurt, who is willing to open her heart to the possibilities of the future when shutting everyone out would be so much easier.'

She squeezed his hands, felt the tears run down her face now.

'We have been through the worst of times together. But because I look at you now and see how much stronger you are—*we* are—and how our love has grown stronger because of it, I know that we can face anything together. And I believe that the best of times are still to come.'

His eyes gleamed, but he cleared his throat and said, 'Mila, I am a different man because of *you*. You've helped me unload the baggage I came into this relationship with. And what I have left I know you'll help me carry.'

He smiled at her, brushed a hair out of her face, and she leaned into his touch.

'I promise to stay with you through good times and bad. I promise to love you with all that is in me and put our relationship first. You mean the world to me, and I can't wait to have a family with you. To show our children what love's supposed to be. No matter what we go through, I will be there for you. Thank you for giving us a second chance.'

They kissed, and she felt it solidify their promises, their declarations of love for each other.

As they walked out of the chapel Mila leaned over to Jordan. 'Do you think this is what your father wanted all along?'

Jordan smiled down at her, and her heart warmed at the look in his eyes. 'Absolutely. And I can't thank him enough.'

She laughed when he scooped her into his arms, and as she placed her head on his shoulder she knew she was finally living the life she had dreamed of.

* * * * *

If you loved this story, don't miss
THE TYCOON'S RELUCTANT CINDERELLA,
the debut novel by Therese Beharrie.
Available now!

If you want to read about another emotional
second-chance romance make sure to indulge in
THE MARRIAGE OF INCONVENIENCE
by Nina Singh.

MILLS & BOON®
Large Print – October 2017

Sold for the Greek's Heir
Lynne Graham

The Prince's Captive Virgin
Maisey Yates

The Secret Sanchez Heir
Cathy Williams

The Prince's Nine-Month Scandal
Caitlin Crews

Her Sinful Secret
Jane Porter

The Drakon Baby Bargain
Tara Pammi

Xenakis's Convenient Bride
Dani Collins

Her Pregnancy Bombshell
Liz Fielding

Married for His Secret Heir
Jennifer Faye

Behind the Billionaire's Guarded Heart
Leah Ashton

A Marriage Worth Saving
Therese Beharrie

MILLS & BOON®
Large Print – November 2017

The Pregnant Kavakos Bride
Sharon Kendrick

The Billionaire's Secret Princess
Caitlin Crews

Sicilian's Baby of Shame
Carol Marinelli

The Secret Kept from the Greek
Susan Stephens

A Ring to Secure His Crown
Kim Lawrence

Wedding Night with Her Enemy
Melanie Milburne

Salazar's One-Night Heir
Jennifer Hayward

The Mysterious Italian Houseguest
Scarlet Wilson

Bound to Her Greek Billionaire
Rebecca Winters

Their Baby Surprise
Katrina Cudmore

The Marriage of Inconvenience
Nina Singh

MILLS & BOON®

Why shop at millsandboon.co.uk?

Each year, thousands of romance readers find their perfect read at millsandboon.co.uk. That's because we're passionate about bringing you the very best romantic fiction. Here are some of the advantages of shopping at www.millsandboon.co.uk:

* **Get new books first**—you'll be able to buy your favourite books one month before they hit the shops

* **Get exclusive discounts**—you'll also be able to buy our specially created monthly collections, with up to 50% off the RRP

* **Find your favourite authors**—latest news, interviews and new releases for all your favourite authors and series on our website, plus ideas for what to try next

* **Join in**—once you've bought your favourite books, don't forget to register with us to rate, review and join in the discussions

Visit **www.millsandboon.co.uk**
for all this and more today!